THE SPACE BETWEEN LOST AND FOUND

Also by Sandy Stark-McGinnis

Extraordinary Birds

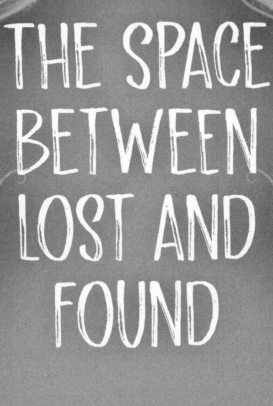

THE SPACE BETWEEN LOST AND FOUND

SANDY STARK-McGINNIS

BLOOMSBURY
CHILDREN'S BOOKS

NEW YORK LONDON OXFORD NEW DELHI SYDNEY

BLOOMSBURY CHILDREN'S BOOKS
Bloomsbury Publishing Inc., part of Bloomsbury Publishing Plc
1385 Broadway, New York, NY 10018

BLOOMSBURY, BLOOMSBURY CHILDREN'S BOOKS, and the Diana logo
are trademarks of Bloomsbury Publishing Plc

First published in the United States of America in April 2020
by Bloomsbury Children's Books

Bloomsbury books may be purchased for business or promotional use.
For information on bulk purchases please contact Macmillan Corporate and
Premium Sales Department at specialmarkets@macmillan.com

Library of Congress Cataloging-in-Publication Data
Names: Stark-McGinnis, Sandy, author.
Title: The space between lost and found / by Sandy Stark-McGinnis.
Description: New York : Bloomsbury, 2020.
Cassie is determined to give her mom—who has early onset Alzheimer's—one last adventure.
Identifiers: LCCN 2020002359 (print) | LCCN 2020002360 (e-book) |
ISBN 978-1-5476-0123-3 (hardcover) • ISBN 978-1-5476-0125-7 (e-book)
Subjects: CYAC: Alzheimer's disease—Fiction. | Family life—Fiction.
Classification: LCC PZ7.1.S73765 Sp 2020 (print) | LCC PZ7.1.S73765 (e-book) |
DDC [Fic]—dc23
LC record available at https://lccn.loc.gov/2020002359
LC e-book record available at https://lccn.loc.gov/2020002360

Book design by Jeanette Levy
Typeset by Westchester Publishing Services
Printed and bound in the U.S.A. by Berryville Graphics Inc., Berryville, Virginia
2 4 6 8 10 9 7 5 3 1

All papers used by Bloomsbury Publishing Plc are natural, recyclable products
made from wood grown in well-managed forests. The manufacturing processes
conform to the environmental regulations of the country of origin.

To find out more about our authors and books visit
www.bloomsbury.com and sign up for our newsletters.

To my mom

THE SPACE BETWEEN LOST AND FOUND

1

This morning I make Mom breakfast, shaping Ritz crackers as close to dolphins as I can. The fins—dorsal and pectoral—and the fluke are hard. The rostrum is, too. I use some Easy Cheese for an eye and for the spots. The dolphin will be a pantropical spotted dolphin. Mom loves dolphins, and she loves Easy Cheese, so there are lots of spots, as many as I can fit.

"Do you want coffee or water? Or do you want something else to drink?" I ask, grabbing a cup from the cupboard.

"Something else."

I open the refrigerator. "We have milk and root beer."

Mom pushes one of her fingers into a single swirl of cheese, lifts it out, and looks at it like it's some strange, new thing before sticking it in her mouth. "That's good."

On the counter, I line up the gallon of milk, the

twelve-ounce bottle of root beer, and a glass of water so she can see all her choices. "Mom, do you want water, milk, coffee, or root beer?" I ask again.

"I'd like something else," she says.

Mom's doctor explained her illness to Dad and me like this: "Let's say you're trying to connect two pieces of paper together with glue. The pieces of paper are brain cells. On the spot where you need to attach them, there are patches of sand and dirt. And when you try to glue the papers, they don't stick."

Another way to explain it is that between my mom's brain cells, fatty tissue has grown, and that fatty tissue prevents the brain cells from connecting.

At the beginning, there were lots of signs she was getting sick: forgetting where she put things, not being able to follow a conversation, not being able to see to the side of her when she drove. One day, she pulled out in front of another car and caused an accident. No one was hurt, but a couple of months later, she quit her job and turned in her driver's license.

She said she was afraid she was going to hurt someone. She said, *"What if I hurt Cassie taking her to school?"*

I decide to give Mom root beer and start eating my breakfast, peanut butter on toast.

"Bottlenose dolphins can swim up to twenty miles an

hour." Mom bites half a cracker. "They can travel almost eighty miles in a day . . . The ocean really is beautiful."

She's staring out the window when she says this, and I'm not sure whether she's mistaking our desert for the ocean, but if she is, it'd make sense. Both are open, deep, and filled with the unknown. Humans are like that, too.

If I had to compare my mom's sickness to either the ocean or to the desert, it'd be more like the ocean. The ocean is an abyss. Like, I could picture myself getting lost in the desert and finding my way back (our desert, at least), but if I ever got lost in the ocean, it'd be harder to find a way home.

The abyss is Alzheimer's disease, and Mom has what's called "early onset." Most people with Alzheimer's get it when they're the age of grandparents or great-grandparents, but Mom is still pretty young, and the doctors say the loss of memory goes faster when it starts early. So time is a big deal. That's why I give Mom root beer and make her Ritz with Easy Cheese for breakfast.

"I wish I could swim in the ocean right now." She eats her last cracker.

I take my plate to the sink. "How 'bout swimming in a pool?" Later, I'll ask Dad if we can take her to the fitness center and let her swim.

She turns away from the window, back to me. "No, the

ocean. You can swim with me. But you don't like to go in deep, do you?"

I take Mom's plate. "No, but I'd go with you, and I might try."

"We'd swim away." Mom grabs my hand, a little too tight. I know she doesn't mean to.

If Dad were here, he would say, "No, you don't want to swim away. You want to stay here at home." He's good at not giving in to Mom's sickness. That's how he keeps going. But I think if imagining herself swimming in the ocean takes her to a different place, somewhere other than here, where she's losing pieces of her memory every day, then that's okay. It gives me comfort in a weird way. It means she's not thinking about what's happening to her.

I put away the Easy Cheese and peanut butter. When I close the cupboard, I hear the front door open. It can't be Dad; he's still getting ready for work. And Mrs. Collins usually yells, "Good morning," as soon as she comes into the house.

I look over at the table, and Mom's not there.

She's reached the sidewalk by the time I catch up to her. "Where are you going?" I ask.

She takes a drink from the bottle of root beer. "I'm just taking a walk," she replies. It's a normal thing to say, the most normal thing she's said in a long time. "I just feel like walking."

4

So that's what we do. We walk down the road. The mornings are still cold, and I realize I didn't have time to grab a jacket. Neither did Mom. Or she didn't remember. "Are you cold?"

"No," she says. "Are you?"

"A little."

"We can walk faster so you can get your blood flowing a little more."

When we get to where the road ends and the desert begins, Mom stops and looks out at the space and the mountains. She folds her arms in front of her chest and takes a deep breath.

"Dolphins," she says, still thinking about the ocean, "can remember sounds. If one of the dolphins from a pod has gone away from the group and doesn't return for years and years, the others will still recognize her sound. They'll remember. Scientists used to think it was elephants that had the longest memory in the animal kingdom—besides humans—but they discovered dolphins can remember even more."

If what she says is true, maybe Mom should go to the ocean and join a pod of dolphins. She'd live with them for so long, she'd turn into one, and maybe her memory would get stronger again.

She steps off the road and onto the desert floor, walking a few steps forward. "Is it supposed to snow?" she asks.

"It could. It snowed in April last year."

"It feels like it will soon." She glances at the cloudy sky.

"Should we try to touch the mountains today?" I ask, because this is the question she'd always ask me before she got sick. From here, the mountains have always looked closer than they actually are. We reach out and try to touch them. Our hands, together, floating in the air, is another moment of normal. She smiles. Her eyes are far away, though, which is a reminder that things aren't really "normal" at all.

"The desert's beautiful," she says. It is.

She turns back, staring at me like I'm the sky. "I know you're my daughter. But I can't remember your name." She holds my face in her hands and presses her forehead against mine, staring into my eyes, searching for "Cassie."

She's been forgetting names of things a lot lately. Like, she'll know a brush is used for fixing your hair but can't remember the word to identify it. Last week, she asked me, "What is that thing you use for writing?"

I found a pencil and a pen. I held up the pencil and said, "This is a pencil." I held up the pen and said, "This is a pen." Mom chose the pen, and then I helped her make a grocery list for Dad.

When she can't remember the name of something, she

describes it to me. "It's a vegetable. It's green. It looks like it has short, dark green hair." Broccoli.

My name is like "pen," "pencil," "broccoli." Except it's not.

I almost say, "This person loves art. She loves to go on hikes. She loves you." But I don't. I can't.

"I'm Cassie." I barely get out the words.

Cassie, I think. *You used to say how beautiful it was. You used to tell me all the time.* And now she can't remember it.

A tear rolls down my cheek. The wind, shaking sagebrush across the desert floor, feels colder. My throat hurts. It's trying to hold the sadness away, sadness mixed with anger, mixed with a wide-open feeling that there isn't anything I, my dad, or even the doctors can do to stop my mom from losing herself. Her memory is like the desert in front of us, formed by tiny particles of mountain broken down into smaller and smaller pieces, becoming sand, then pieces of sand breaking down so tiny, they don't exist anymore.

Except, in the desert, it seems like there are always more pieces of sand to replace those that are lost. Once Mom loses a memory, it sometimes doesn't come back. So the chances of her ever remembering my name again aren't good.

"Isn't it beautiful?" she says again.

No. Nothing is beautiful. How can she say that when

she can't remember my name? My name is beautiful, remember? She's the one who gave it to me. How could she forget?

I want to scream across the "beautiful" desert, but I have to remind myself that Mom can't help what's happening to her.

I take a deep breath, trying to swallow my tears, and bend down to collect some rocks. I use my hand to scrape the ground, making the dirt flat and more compact, and use the rocks to spell out my name. If I had paint, I'd paint them blue, ocean blue, so Mom could get lost in the letters.

"See." I press myself against her and feel her warmth, erasing the cold wind for a second.

I'm hoping she'll read the word, but instead she takes a last drink of her root beer and kisses me on the nose. "I love you."

That should be enough. *I love you.*

But on the way back to the house, I can't help but repeat "Cassie" over and over again, the rhythm of my name dictating our steps.

Saying it out loud probably won't help her remember my name. But I need to hear it. Sometimes I need help, too.

"Cassie." Dad's waiting for us inside the doorway. "Where did you go?"

Mom slips under his arm into the house and leaves the empty root beer bottle on the porch.

"Mom wanted to go for a walk, and I followed her."

He doesn't like that answer. "I'm going to tell you again. We can't let her walk out the door on her own. It makes our lives harder. Okay?"

I nod. I agree that Mom escaping and going outside does make our lives harder, but I can't blame her for wanting to escape.

I get that he's afraid. I am, too. But our fears have different degrees, different angles and values when it comes to Mom. I'm afraid we won't have time to do and say everything we need to before we have to say goodbye.

Sometimes Dad's fears really have to do with how people would react to Mom if we did take her places, but he says he's just focused on keeping her safe.

This is the complete opposite of our life before Mom got sick. We would go places all the time, hiking, camping, taking trips to the beach.

"We just went for a walk, Dad. That's all. I stayed with her the whole time. Everything was fine." I grab the root beer bottle and go to my room.

I shove the bottle and my math book into my backpack. "Cassie," I whisper. "It's Cassie."

On a shelf, there's a container with small plastic dolphins

that Mom gave me last year for Christmas. I grab three, not caring what kinds of dolphins they are, and shove them inside my jeans' pocket.

There's a knock on the front door. "Good morning!" Mrs. Collins says.

It's not a good morning.

———————

On the way to school, it starts to rain. The radio plays; Dad's listening to the news. I swear I hear the newswoman say, "Up next, a story about a woman who can't remember her own daughter's name."

Mom was the one who used to drive me to school and pick me up. I miss my rides with her. She was good at making the twenty minutes fun.

"So," Dad says, "do you want to have spaghetti for dinner tonight?"

"That's fine."

"Spaghetti's your favorite."

"It is."

From the car window, I can see the mountains. They're a shade of red, like the ones Georgia O'Keeffe painted. I've been saving my money to go to Santa Fe and visit her museum. It would be nice to get lost in her red cliffs and *The Lawrence Tree* or hide behind cow skulls or inside one of her sunflower paintings.

Dad pulls up in front of Desert Valley Elementary School. I get out, lift my too-heavy backpack from the back seat, and close the door.

"Cassie?" He says my name like a question. He's been doing this a lot since Mom got sick. I get it, though. I feel unsure about a lot of things now, too. Questions and the unknown are our new normal.

I lean against the open window.

"Is something wrong?"

"No."

"Okay." Of course, Dad knows there's something wrong, something besides just Mom, and he says *okay* because he thinks if he doesn't pressure me about it, I'll be more likely to tell him. But I don't want to say anything. He has enough to worry about.

"Have a good day," he says.

I wave goodbye. A "good day" would look like this: walking through the door when I get home and Mom saying, "Cassie, did you do your homework?" or, "Cassie, please clean up your room," or, "Cassie, will you take out the garbage?"

Or just, "Cassie."

SWIMMING THE ENGLISH CHANNEL

The wind is perfect, and we're the only ones on the beach.

"You ready to run?" Dad asks.

Mom gives me the reel. "You're ready."

But I know how much she loves to fly kites. "You first."

"Together." She grins and takes my hand.

Behind us, Dad holds the kite in the air. "You'll go on three."

Against my feet, the sand is cool. I usually look ahead and try to listen to Dad give directions, but Mom runs with her eyes on the kite. I don't know how she does it. Lots of practice, maybe? Or a trust that her feet are going to land where they're supposed to, even if she isn't focused on planting them with each step.

"Let's give it some slack, Cassie," she says.

I roll more string out from the reel and try to look up at the kite, too. My feet stumble a little, and I fall, letting go of the string on my way down. Mom holds on and keeps running.

"You okay?" Her voice travels down the beach.

"I'm fine." I am, except for a little taste of sunscreen in my mouth. (Mom says, with our pale skin, we need to be extra careful.) I don't bother getting up and open my eyes to the sky. There's no sun to shield them from, and I can watch the clouds. They're moving fast today.

Pretty soon, her shoulder is right beside mine. "Okay, what ocean animals do you see?" She points up at one of the clouds, to the left of the kite, still flying. "That's definitely a stingray."

I can't make out the outline of a stingray at all. "I don't see it."

"Keep looking. It's there."

I try to find it but can't. "You know, the truth is, I usually can't find half the things you say you see in the clouds." I laugh.

"Well, Cassie." Mom raises up on her elbows, leans over, and gives me a kiss on the cheek. "The truth is, I make up half the things I say I see in the clouds."

I smile. "I know."

She lies back down, grabs my hand, and sets it over her heart, while her other hand holds the reel. "I guess it's not exactly telling the truth, is it? It's nice of you to play along."

"It is nice of me, huh?"

Mom giggles. "I do it for a good reason, and I suppose you know what the reason is, too?"

"Maybe because you want to keep the game going longer?"

I wait for her to tell me whether I'm right, but Dad walks up. "You want me to take the kite?" he asks.

"No, I got it." Mom stares up at the colors. The kite bobs and weaves with the wind, but for the most part, it stays steady.

Last year in math class, Mrs. Jones, my teacher, asked us if we could identify characteristics of a kite. *They're different colors and different shapes.* That's all I knew. When she started talking about adjacent and perpendicular lines, I understood what she was teaching us, but I didn't want to think too much about it. Because I like to think of kites the way Mom does: *an extension of our arms. With them, we can touch the sky.*

"Dad, do you see a stingray in the clouds?" I ask him, pointing to where Mom did earlier.

Mom laughs.

"I know that trick," Dad says.

The reel of the kite drops onto her stomach, but then the wind scoots it across the beach toward the ocean. All of us get up and run after it. By the time we reach the reel, the kite has tumbled onto the sand, the tide washing over it. Mom picks it up by the frame.

"Not much use now," I say.

"I don't know." She shakes the kite gently. "Let's dry it out and see what happens. It's always worth a try."

"It's not going to . . ." Dad stops himself from saying "work" because Mom's giving him a look. It's one she gives me when I'm about to complain about getting a B on a math test.

I know what she's going to say next. It's her answer for pretty much everything, and she says it in a soft voice that sounds even quieter compared to the waves. "Let's go get some ice cream. We can talk about how we're going to get this kite back up into the air over a sundae."

Dad says he'll meet us at the car.

Before leaving, it's my and Mom's tradition to always say goodbye to the ocean. "Until next time," she says, and waves to the water between us and the horizon. "I'm always amazed at how big it is."

"Me too." We lift our feet out of the damp sand and move closer to the water. "How far do you think you'd be able to swim out before you started to get scared?"

"Pretty far."

Even though the water would be cold, Mom would keep swimming. She'd only stop if she got hungry or thirsty.

"What about you?" she asks as she holds my hand.

"Not very far." I'm a good swimmer, but I don't like swimming in the ocean.

"Why not?"

"It's scary. All that space around you, and it's dark and unpredictable."

" 'Unpredictable.' That's a big word."

"That's why I like math. Numbers. They have a pattern."

Mom laughs. "Patterns are good, but what if 'unpredictable' leads to amazing adventures?"

"If I had to jump in the ocean first to get to that adventure, well, I'd rather sit down on the beach and do long division all day."

A car horn sounds. Dad's waving for us to *come on*. "Ice cream!" he yells. "Rocky road! Orange sherbet! Chocolate chip!" Each flavor one of our favorites.

"We better go."

Mom points to the sky. "There's a dolphin."

The cloud does have a dolphin-like shape to it. "I see it this time," I say.

She moves her foot back and forth across the sand.

"What's the longest distance you've ever swam?" I ask her.

"I'm not sure. But one day I'm going to swim the English Channel," she says. Mom loves big ideas. I haven't heard this plan before, but I'm not too surprised.

"Maybe by then you'll see the water in a different

way . . . or maybe you'll still think it's scary. But it doesn't matter . . . unless you want to join me."

"I don't think so," I say.

"That's okay. Because when I swim it, I'll need a support crew!" She nods and gives me a wink. "You're good at reading charts and data, so you can be in charge of reporting any rough weather or crazy currents that could push me off course."

I laugh as we grab our flip-flops.

When we get to the end of the sand, I hear Dad. There are only two other cars in the parking lot. On ours, all the doors are open, and he's sitting on the hood, leaning back against the front windshield, sunglasses on, singing, "Everybody Wants to Rule the World," a song from when he was young.

Mom and I sing with him—we know the words by heart. Mom dances around to the other side of the car and takes his hand. It's not really a song to dance to, but they dance anyway.

She waves for me to join them. I'm not going to dance, but Mom says that's okay, and I believe her.

I keep singing, though, and change the words to "Everybody wants to eat ice cream!"

Dad raises his arms in the air. "Yes! Ice cream!"

Mom will choose orange sherbet. Dad, rocky road. Me, chocolate chip.

The song fades, but the next one on the playlist is "Girls Just Want to Have Fun."

"Ice cream can wait just a few more minutes," Mom says and strikes a Cyndi Lauper pose, the one on the *She's So Unusual* album. One year for her birthday, Dad bought her a poster of the cover. It hangs in the office at home.

"Come on." She dances over to me. "You have to dance."

"No way."

"Yes, you do. It's a beautiful day. You're at the beach. You're about to go get ice cream. You—*we*—have every reason to dance."

"I'll just sing, thanks." But she's getting to me a little, and I find myself tapping one of my feet.

"How can you listen to this song without dancing?" Mom twirls around me.

"The same way I can look at the ocean and not want to swim in it."

"Cassie Rodrigues!" she shouts over the music, over the waves, over the space that is blue and wide and perfect. "I'll make you a bet. When I finish swimming the English Channel, you have to dance with me to this song. Deal?"

"Deal." I hold out my hand, and we shake on it.

2

Since it's a rainy-day schedule, I go right to my classroom. I'm the first one here.

Mrs. G is just opening the Chromebook cart. "Good morning, Cassie."

"Good morning, Mrs. G." I sit down, and it's quiet except for the sound of the rain. Mrs. G keeps the back door of the room open for kids coming from the cafeteria. Opening my sketchbook, I wait for images to come to me like they used to, images of starry nights and trees that touch the sky and kites flying over the ocean. Things I used to draw. But when Mom's memory started to fade, so did my ideas.

Still, I force myself to sketch something new, pressing the pencil to the paper, drawing two lines for legs, bent at the knees, two for arms with right angles at the elbows, a line for the torso, and a circle for the head.

I draw shoes on the stick figure, give it some shorts and a T-shirt, and sketch motion lines behind it so the figure at least appears to be moving. But I could draw a billion motion lines, and this person would still be stuck in place.

I look over my shoulder at a poster Mrs. G has hanging on the wall by her desk. There's a picture of a bike with a quote by Albert Einstein: "Life is like riding a bicycle. To keep your balance, you must keep moving."

I can't even remember the last time I rode my bike.

A group of kids walks in, and the classroom gets louder, which is fine by me. I unzip my backpack and take out the plastic root beer bottle. As other students get busy playing board games, I walk to the open back door and set the bottle out in the rain.

I don't know if people inherit feelings from their moms and dads, but if they do, I definitely got my love of rain from my mom. I also inherited her eyes, her mouth, and the color of her hair.

By the time the first bell rings, rainwater has filled the bottle only a quarter of the way. Back inside, I use a paper towel to dry the outside, then twist the lid on and stuff it in my backpack.

During morning announcements, I take out the dolphins I have in my pocket. One is a spinner, the other a bottlenose.

"Art Club," one of the student council members says over the intercom, *"will be meeting today after school in room twelve. Mrs. G says she has exciting news to share."*

With a black Sharpie I keep in my desk, I write my name across both dolphins' flukes.

The last time Mrs. G shared exciting news with Art Club, an artist came to talk to us and brought in some pieces of her work. She was a sculptor. Bailey and I didn't have sculpting clay, but we went home and mixed mud from the red dirt behind her house and used it to make mini sculptures of animals.

Mrs. G says, "Good morning," to the whole class and asks us to get out our math journals and math books.

I slide the two dolphins into my pocket and dig in my desk, taking out my box filled with charcoal pencils and pushing aside all the empty chip bags, crumpled papers (some graded that I've never taken home, but then, Dad has stopped asking about them anyway), and other things in there.

There must be a Guinness World Record for how much stuff someone can cram into a desk. I'd easily break it, because I'm a collector, another thing I inherited from Mom. If I had to estimate, I'd say there are at least twenty pencils of different sizes, plus pieces of eraser and a bunch of things I've found on the playground. Once, I found a silver lighter that didn't work. It had a lion on it, and it looked old and fancy. I turned that one in to the office, because it looked like something someone didn't want to lose.

My most valuable possession at the moment is a water bottle with a highlighter cap that I've glued to the top and pieces of pink eraser stuck to the body. If someone ever asks me what it is, I'd say, "I don't know. It just looks weird."

And weird is my existence. The world is upside down, so why not sneak all the erasers from the extra-eraser container and glue them to a paper to make a picture of a sun or a house with a fence, or pour Elmer's glue into a water bottle I've cut in half to make a glue cylinder?

"Before we get started on math," Mrs. G says, "I'm passing out art show flyers for you to take home. If you're interested in submitting something, all the information is here."

I find my book under two empty bags of Takis, both of them falling on the floor as I slide it out.

Mrs. G hands me a flyer. "I still think about the art piece you entered last year, Cassie," she says. "Can't wait to see what you create this time."

Last May was right before Mom got diagnosed, when making art was easy. But now I want to tell Mrs. G she might be disappointed, because she only has stick figures to look forward to.

I leave the flyer on my desk and grab the Taki bags. Walking to the garbage, which is on the other side of the room by the sink, I pass Bailey's desk. She turns around to put a flyer in her backpack and catches me staring. I wave hello, but she has on her fierce, don't-bother-me look, the same one she used on the other team every time we played soccer. She told me once it was her Wonder Woman / Joan of Arc look. It was always one of the things I liked about Bailey, but something feels different when it's pointed at me.

She turns back around, and I throw away the Taki bags.

"Okay." Mrs. G claps her hands together. She does this when she's excited to share something with us. "We've added decimals, we've subtracted decimals, we've multiplied decimals, and today we're going to . . ."

The whole class responds. "Divide decimals."

"Dividing decimals is my favorite." Mrs. G picks up a marker. "Anyone want to guess why?"

Charlie Ward raises his hand. Our teacher zigzags among desks and stands in the middle of the room.

"Maybe you like division—Mrs. G, don't take this the wrong way—because you like to break things?" Some of the students laugh.

"Well, if by *things* you mean numbers, then I'd have to say you're right, Charlie." She zigzags her way back to the front of the classroom. "What is the purpose of division?

I'm going to give you a minute to think about that question, and then I'll choose someone to answer."

What is the purpose of division? Mrs. G asked this question for all the operations. I think the purpose of division would be the opposite of the purpose of multiplication.

Mrs. G rings her Zen singing bowl. She waits for the sound to end. She told us it reminds her of desert highways that go on forever. She chooses a Popsicle stick with one of our names on it out of a container. "Susan, what do you think?"

Susan Taylor sits right next to Bailey, who is slouched in her chair, staring down at her math book.

"Well," Susan says, "the purpose of division is to see how many times a small number can go into a greater number. Like if you had a dollar—which is equal to one hundred pennies—and you wanted to buy pieces of bubble gum that each cost twenty-five cents, you'd use division to help you figure out how many pieces of gum you could buy by figuring out how many times twenty-five goes into a hundred."

"Thank you, Susan. Now, another question." Mrs. G loves to ask us questions. She writes "100" on the whiteboard. "What is happening to the hundred when you're figuring out how many times twenty-five goes into it?"

I raise my hand, but she calls on Austin Lopez. "You're breaking the hundred into four parts."

"Yes." Mrs. G claps her hands again. "So what's the *purpose* of division?"

A few students, including me, forget to raise their hands and call out, "To break down a number!"

"Right!" Mrs. G draws a line from the "100" she wrote on the board to a box. Inside the box, she writes "25." She draws three more lines and three more boxes to show the four groups of twenty-five. "Now, Susan mentioned that when we divide, we're taking a greater number and seeing how many times a smaller number can go into it, and that's true. Even if we have a dividend—the number we're dividing up—that's smaller than the divisor—the number we're dividing by—we can still calculate the quotient."

Mrs. G writes the equation "1 divided by 100 =," which is actually something we've done before.

I know one divided by one hundred can be written as one over one hundred, which is the same as one hundredth.

"On three, I want everyone to tell me the quotient for one divided by one hundred." Mrs. G counts to three on her fingers.

"One hundredth!" the class says.

"So," Andrea Gutierrez says, "Mrs. G, what we just did is break up the number one into a hundred pieces, right?"

"Yes." Mrs. G has a big smile on her face. "And each of those pieces has a value of . . ." She stops and writes "0.01" on the board. "This is what makes division and decimals magical, in my opinion. You can break down the smallest of numbers into the minutest of parts. And I think that is pretty cool."

Some students laugh, and Mrs. G goes over the goal of the lesson and gives us practice problems.

I do a couple with Mrs. G, then go ahead and start doing the problems in our workbook. I get lost in the numbers, breaking them down to the tiniest of parts.

Our place value chart only goes to the millionths place, but I know there are place values after that, billionths and trillionths and more, and it makes me wonder how small numbers can be broken down and whether they can be broken down so much, they don't exist anymore, or whether it's possible that numbers, unlike memories, never disappear.

3

There's a bench on the edge of the soccer field that's my regular spot at recess. I open my bag of chili lime Takis, set it next to me, and turn my sketchbook to the page where I'd drawn the stick figures. I draw talking bubbles above their heads and write division equations like the ones we did in math: 4.6 divided by 8, 7.2 divided by 12.

I tap my pencil against the paper. In the middle of the page, I sketch a kite with a tail and a reel, floating over waves—the English Channel. An arm rises from the water: my mom, swimming, her fingers open like she just let go of the string.

I shade in the kite with my pencil. If numbers can be broken down into the smallest of parts, I wonder if memories can be, too. I draw the string down so that it wraps around one of Mom's fingers. I extend the perpendicular lines of the kite and connect them point to point, making a frame around it. In the spaces between the lines, I write my name.

I call these my "memory sketches." I draw another one, Mom on the hiking trail this time, ahead of her a sign sticking out of the water: PIKE'S TRAIL—10 MILES. In the background, I sketch a mountain, and on the peak, I sketch another sign: CASSIE'S NAME IS HERE.

I reach down for some more Takis and tear the paper out of my book, wadding it up. This isn't going to help.

The nearest garbage can is by the snack area. Kids stand near it eating their Cheez-Its, potato chips, granola bars. As I make my way over, I see Bailey. She's standing with a group of friends, eating Takis like me. She's wearing red tennis shoes, soccer socks pulled up to the bottoms of her knees, long red shorts, and a T-shirt to match. Bailey's hard to miss.

She and her friends stand in a perfect circle. They talk and laugh every once in a while, and sometimes they turn and look at something that's happening on the playground.

What I know about circles: they don't have corners, they are 360 degrees, and their radius is a measurement from the center to the outside edge. Finding the area of a circle has something to do with pi. If I were invited to join the circle, it would change the radius, the diameter, and the area—everything about it would shift.

Even though I'm bad at basketball, I stop about five steps away from the garbage can and attempt to toss the wadded-up paper inside. It hits the edge, of course, and falls to the ground next to the pair of red tennis shoes I know so well.

Bailey's frozen, like a stick figure. She doesn't give me her Wonder Woman / Joan of Arc. She doesn't give me any look at all. I don't blame her. There's a second when I have a chance to tell her I'm sorry. I owe her at least an apology. But words are like my art; they don't come easy now, either. Before I can grab the paper from the ground, she takes off to the soccer field.

It wasn't that long ago that Bailey and I spent every Saturday playing soccer. If we didn't have a game, I'd ride my bike to her house, and we'd stop at the grocery store and buy Gatorade and sunflower seeds and head to the park. We stayed there for hours. If we got tired of kicking the ball around, we climbed the dome, sitting at the top, or found shade under a tree, spitting sunflower seed shells into our empty bottles as we talked.

I watch Bailey now on the field, weaving in and out of the defenders. She hasn't lost any of her skills. They look sharper. I wonder if she still goes to the park on her own.

I walk along the edge of the field, grabbing my bag from the bench and walking to the water fountain. In front of me, hanging on the wall, is a poster: Open House Student Art Show, May 18th, 5:00 to 7:00 pm. Under pictures of a paintbrush, a palette, and a sketch pencil, there is more information in smaller writing. All student art is due by Friday, May 12th. You may submit art to your teacher or to the school office. We encourage all students to enter.

Last year, before my mom started to get really sick, I sketched a portrait of her and entered it in the show.

If I entered something this year, it'd probably have to be a portrait of a stick person; or—since all forms of art are accepted—I could dig the wadded-up paper I just threw away out of the garbage and paint it blue and green, a representation of Earth with the stick figures buried inside; or I could paint it gold and title it *Fool's Gold*; or paint it white and title it *The Disappearance*.

Or maybe I could paint it white and black and call it *Soccer Ball*.

The bell rings. I go back to the garbage can. The wad of paper is buried under some Cheez-Its and mini Oreo cookie wrappers. I grab it.

Marissa Lucas, one of Bailey's friends, laughs. "You looking for some more snacks?"

I know she's joking, but I pretend it's a serious question. "No, my stomach's full, thanks. I lost something and found it." I hold up the wadded paper and go line up for class.

So does Marissa. She smiles and waves to Bailey, who's standing about five students ahead of me. Bailey glances back, and I dribble the wad of paper with my knees like it's a soccer ball.

"Cassie," Mrs. G says. "Recess is over."

I stop dribbling the paper. Bailey's back is turned toward me, but now she knows that I still have my soccer skills, too.

Instead of shoving the paper in my desk, I smooth it out as much as I can, fold it in half, and stick it in my math book to try and flatten it out more. Maybe it's the start of something.

The first time I ever talked to Bailey, we were outside painting self-portraits. Bailey was painting a soccer ball on her shirt, and I was doing my best to draw a Georgia O'Keeffe sunflower I'd just seen in an art book. I painted it in the sky, upside down, the stem hanging from one cloud, and when a parent volunteer asked, "Shouldn't the flowers be closer to the ground?" Bailey said, "It's a floating flower," like floating flowers were something she saw all the time.

Today we're waiting in Mrs. G's room for the Art Club meeting. When the last two kids arrive, Mrs. G says, "Our club has been given a wonderful opportunity, and it will take all of us working together to make it special and unique."

"Are we going to paint the school?" Jonathan Mitchell asks.

"Not exactly," Mrs. G says. "We're going to paint a mural for the art show. So today, before we leave, I want us to come up with a theme."

I raise my hand. "How 'bout an ocean theme?"

"We live in the desert," Jonathan says.

I don't see why that means we can't draw an ocean. Mom would really like it. If Dad let her come to the show, anyway. "That would make it all the more unique, right?" Compared to the ocean, which is filled with life and movement, the desert is empty and too still.

Jonathan shrugs. "I just think we need to make it something that connects to our school. And our school mascot is a coyote, so maybe we should make a background where we can include coyotes."

"I like the desert idea," says Bailey. "The ocean wouldn't make sense for us. Like Jonathan said, we're surrounded by the desert. It's where we live, so I think it would mean more to students if we painted the desert. Didn't Georgia O'Keeffe think the desert was beautiful?"

"I think she was talking about the land that surrounded her house." I don't look up at Bailey. There was a time when I could have depended on her to vote for my idea. But I forgot she knows and loves Georgia O'Keeffe just as much as I do, and that is something that still connects us.

"But the land around her house was desert, right?" Bailey asks.

"Yeah," I whisper. "Yeah, she was talking about the desert."

Bailey's favorite Georgia O'Keeffe paintings were always the skulls. She thought they looked cool, but she also liked that they reminded her of life in some way. Mine are the red cliff landscapes where she mixed warm and cool colors. When Bailey first asked me why they were my favorite, I said, "The colors are honest. They make me feel sad and happy at the same time."

Mrs. G asks if there are any other suggestions. No one raises their hand. "Well, we can make a decision now, or I can give you time to think about other ideas and we can vote next week. I want this to be the club's decision so you'll be more inspired."

I expect Bailey to say that two people voted for the

desert and only one for the ocean, but instead she says, "How 'bout we vote now but include a third choice of 'think about it'?" I shoot her a smile, but I'm not sure she sees it.

"Great idea," Mrs. G says. She writes "Ocean," "Desert," and "Think about it" on the board. I'm surprised when Bailey and everyone else except for Jonathan votes for "Think about it."

Mrs. G walks over to the back door. "I want to show you where we'll be presenting the mural. You're going to need not only your creative skills for this project but your math skills as well."

She glances at me and waves for the club to follow her outside. She unlocks a supply room near the cafeteria and shows us a long, rectangular chalkboard with wheels. "We'll paint panels of butcher paper, and then we'll mount them so they cover the green chalkboard part. The mural will be displayed at the entrance of the art show."

I visualize a sea of cool colors filling the space, with dolphins and stingrays swimming in blue.

"How do you think Georgia O'Keeffe would've painted the ocean?" Bailey's standing behind me.

"I don't know," I say. "Desert and ocean are different worlds, right?"

"Yeah. She definitely would've done it her way."

True. Mrs. G starts to dismiss us. "Remember, start thinking of ideas, even sketching some to show the club. I'll see you next week."

I head to the after-school program in the cafeteria. I've always gone because both Mom and Dad were working, and even though Mrs. Collins and Mom are at home now, Dad and I both thought I should stay, to keep part of my normal routine. Normal is good.

Part of what Georgia O'Keeffe gets about the desert is its sparseness. She couldn't have done that with the ocean. The ocean has too many layers, too much depth.

———————

While everyone else finishes homework, I stand by one of the doors. It's raining again, so I fill the rest of my plastic bottle.

The rain falls hard, and the bottle fills up fast. I pour a little of it out so the water doesn't overflow when I twist on the cap, then take it to one of the tables.

From my pocket, I take out the plastic dolphins. I push one of them through the opening at the top of the bottle, but its pectoral fins get stuck, so I have to work one fin in at a time before it dives into the rainwater. I do the same for the other dolphin, then twist the cap back on.

"What did you make today, Cassie?" Jessica asks. She's

one of the after-school teachers. It's better than her asking me if I want to play a game and then trying to find another student to play, too. I know she worries about how I'm always spending time by myself.

I hold up the bottle and rock it back and forth just enough to make the dolphins swim. "It's for my mom."

"You know, you could add some blue dye to the water; then it would really look like the ocean." Jessica likes to make suggestions.

"Maybe just a little." If I added too much, the dolphins would be hard to see. And the whole point is to see the dolphins.

I spot my dad walking through the cafeteria doors. It's only four thirty. He's early.

"Looks like it's time for you to go home," Jessica says.

Home. It's weird how the meaning of a word can change in such a short period of time. For me, there's the home before Mom got sick and the one now.

I slide the water bottle into the netted pocket of my backpack and follow Dad out the door.

"You're not supposed to be here yet."

"Yeah, it was slow at work."

I don't believe him. I think he was worried about me from this morning, and he made it so he could come pick me up now.

"How was your day?" he asks.

"Good."

Outside, he takes a detour to get a drink of water. When he stands up, he sees the art show flyer. He points at it. "What are you entering this year?"

"Um, I'm still trying to figure that out." Dad doesn't have to know that I'm not planning on entering at all. "I'm sure I'll come up with something, though."

"Yes." He kisses me on top of my head. "You will. I'd like to see it when you're finished."

"You'll be the first one I show it to." If I make something at all.

"What medium?" he asks.

I pretend to not hear him. "What?"

"Medium. Charcoal, or are you painting this year? Acrylic or watercolor?"

"I just don't want to do the same thing I did last year."

I open the car door.

My foot crushes a pink doughnut box. Dad must've stopped by Family Donuts to buy a couple apple fritters to eat on the way to work this morning.

I scoot the box to the side. It reminds me of the Saturday Dad and Mom woke me up at five in the morning to take me to an art museum where there was a special Georgia O'Keeffe exhibit. We stopped for doughnuts on the way.

Back then, Dad liked surprises because they made Mom happy. She could find a way to surprise us just by going to the grocery store. She'd sneak a gallon of vanilla ice cream, some chocolate syrup, and whipped cream into the shopping basket when we weren't looking, hiding them under the rest of the food so we couldn't see them until we were at the register. "Come on—you can't pass on ice-cream sundaes, right?" she'd ask Dad, knowing he couldn't.

As soon as Dad turns the ignition, heat blows on high through the vents. He tries to make it as warm as he can inside the truck, like the warmth is a blanket we both can use until we get home.

He plays the radio low, songs from when he was young. It's better than the news.

Whenever Mom, Dad, and I went somewhere together, they used to sing along. We were happy. Mom could remember words to the songs—she could remember everything. And there wasn't a day that went by when she wouldn't say to me, "I love you, Cassie. You and your dad are the world to me."

Now she lives in her own world, and sometimes it's hard to tell whether Dad and I live in that world with her.

"I said we'd have spaghetti tonight, didn't I?" Dad brings me back to the present.

"You did."

He pulls in front of our house but doesn't turn off the engine. "I'm going to go to the grocery store to get some sauce. We can let Mrs. Collins leave early today, too."

"Can't Mom and I come with you? I'll stay by her the whole time."

"It's easier if I go by myself." He leans over and opens my door for me. "It's a quick trip, anyway. I'm only getting a couple things."

I understand that it's *easier* to leave Mom at home, but it's not what she would want. She has always loved being outside and going places.

But it's not up to me. I lift my backpack out of the truck and walk toward our house.

4

When I open the front door, the bottom scrapes something against the floor. I stop short. Broken pieces of glass and ceramics are scattered across the living room.

Mom's watching a nature show. An image of birds flying fills the TV screen. There's a bag of Doritos and a couple of empty cans of root beer on the floor next to her chair.

"Mrs. Collins!" I tiptoe around the scattered pieces that are on the floor. "Are you okay?"

"Yes!" Mrs. Collins comes from the kitchen with a broom and a dustpan. "I'm so sorry, Cassie. I was doing laundry and heard glass breaking. Your mom just started throwing them on the floor. I couldn't stop her."

The shelf where Mom keeps her dolphin collection and the shells and sand dollars she and I have collected on our vacations is empty.

"I don't know what made her do this." Mrs. Collins starts sweeping pieces into the dustpan. "She was watching TV; then I went to put some clothes in the dryer, and I heard the sound. I'm so sorry."

"It's okay." I reach out for the broom. "I'll finish cleaning up. You can go ahead and leave."

"You sure?" Mrs. Collins holds the dustpan. "I can help you."

"No, it's okay. We'll see you tomorrow. Thank you, Mrs. Collins."

I bend down and examine a blue pectoral fin. I'd estimate close to a hundred pieces are scattered across the floor. Some dolphins are salvageable; I can put them back together. Mom's collection might go from thirty to fifteen, and some of the dolphins might look funny—a blue glass fin glued to a white ceramic body with a rainbow-colored fluke, maybe—but I can fix it.

Not the sand dollars, though. I pick up the pieces, careful so they don't break more. Whenever we went on a sand dollar treasure hunt, Mom used to carry a pack around her waist lined with napkins to put them in. "They're good luck," she'd remind me, "but only if you find whole ones. They can't be chipped or have a crack in them, either." The best place to find luck was Martin's Beach. That's where all the sand dollars on the shelf were from.

Footsteps slide across the floor behind me, and Mom bends down, starting to pick up pieces of sand dollars, too, placing them in my hand.

"Remember when we found these?" I ask.

She rubs her fingers over a piece, like she does remember. "They brought us luck for a long time," she says.

"I'll be right back." In the kitchen, I scrape the pieces into a small container. I guess our luck ran out.

For a long time, I didn't know sand dollars were living things. Then we found one that looked like it had black fur all over it. "We can't take that one!" Mom had said, reaching for it. Then she threw it into the ocean, as far as she could. "It's still alive."

"What do you mean, *alive*?" I'd asked. "I thought they were just shells."

"Oh, no." Mom kissed me on the forehead. "They're living creatures, sweetie. Very much so."

It was kind of weird to realize. She'd continued walking down the beach. "Life shows up in the strangest of things."

When I bring the container out to where Mom is, she's no longer picking up pieces. She's by the shelf, gently waving a whole sand dollar up in the air, smiling like she's caught the moon. "We still have a little luck . . . ," she says, her eyes holding a trace of her old self.

"Where'd you find that?"

She points to the shelf. "Guess it didn't make it to the floor." She's talking like the breaking just occurred, like she didn't do it herself. But at least there's a part of her that recognizes something happened.

"Can I see?" I ask. It lies flat on her hand. I don't pick it up. Instead, I cup my hand over hers and close my eyes and make a wish on what *little luck* we still have. *Please remember my name.*

The front door opens. "What happened?" Dad looks across the floor, at the shattered pieces I meant to finish cleaning up before he came home.

He isn't careful about where he steps. Pieces of glass dolphins crunch under his shoes as he drops the bag of spaghetti on the couch and grabs the broom. "This is why we can't take your mom anywhere—because she does this kind of stuff. Cassie, why aren't you cleaning this up?" He whispers bad words under his breath.

"I'm sorry." I reach out to take the broom from him. "I can finish cleaning and then start dinner. Don't worry about it, okay?"

"No, I'll do it!" His hands shake as he sweeps pieces into the dustpan. He starts toward the kitchen to the garbage can under the sink.

"Don't throw them away, please." From one of the cupboards, I grab a bowl we use for popcorn and hold it out so Dad can dump the pieces inside.

"You don't want these, Cassie," he says.

"Yes, I do."

"They're useless now."

"No, they're not. They're pieces."

"They're broken pieces. What are you going to do with them?"

I grab the handle of the dustpan. "I'm going to put them back together," I say.

"Cassie, even if you are able to magically put these pieces back together, there's a good chance your mom will break them again."

But he doesn't resist as I lift the dustpan's handle and slide the pieces into the bowl. "Then I'll put them together again." I understand Dad's point. I hope he gets mine.

While he finishes cleaning up, I start dinner. I fill a pot with water, light one of the burners, and grab spaghetti and a jar of sauce from a cupboard.

"We should just make sandwiches tonight. It'll be easier."

"No, it's okay. I've already started the water. I can make it."

"Thank you," he says and takes a deep breath. I know he gets frustrated. I know he's tired, too.

A few minutes later, I hear water running through the pipes. He's taking a shower.

I set the table, then cut some bread and throw it in

the toaster oven. I pour lettuce from a bag onto three plates, wash some tomatoes, and get the ranch salad dressing from the refrigerator.

While I wait for the water to boil, I take the bowl of dolphin pieces to my room. Sitting on my desk, in the spot where I do homework, is the sand dollar Mom found on the shelf.

Above my desk is a poster. The top half shows the sky, the middle is the horizon line and calm water, and then under the water are different ocean fish and shades of light and dark. I remember the day I walked into my room and Mom was standing on my chair, holding pushpins in her hand. "This is a good one for your room, right? I know how much you like the ocean."

"Sure, it's fine." I didn't want to tell her that the ocean scares me. I love searching for shells and sand dollars and exploring tide pools, but I'd never swim in the water. I'm not brave like Mom is. I'd think too much about how much space there is around me and how I can't see where I'm going.

"You never got scared when you did ocean swims?" I'd asked her.

She'd pushed one more pin in the bottom right-hand corner of the poster and turned to me. "I was too focused on my stroke. Every once in a while, I'd start thinking about how cold the water was, but I knew if I thought about it too much, I wouldn't finish." Then she squeezed my shoulders. "Swimming in the ocean isn't for everyone, but you might want to try someday. We'll go together, and I'll be right beside you."

Dad told me when Mom got sick that our world was going to be dictated by her, that she was going to be the one who controlled what we did and how we did it, and that was just the way it was going to have to be.

He didn't mean it in a bad way. He meant it in the most honest way possible. But this wasn't anything new for me. My life has always been dictated by my mom, sometimes in bad ways but mostly good.

And someday she won't be here.

I move the tip of my finger through the broken pieces and find two fins and a fluke. Gorilla Glue will be best for this project. I twist off the lid. I glue one of the dolphins together and go check the pot.

At dinner, we all sit at our regular spots. Mom's by the window so she can look out onto the desert and the mountains.

"Food looks good," Dad says to me. "Thank you."

We start eating, except Mom can't get the spaghetti to stay on the fork. It keeps slipping off before she can get it to her mouth. She tries hooking one string at a time onto one of the prongs, but that slips off, too.

On Mom's fourth try, Dad reaches over to show her

how to roll the spaghetti, but she pushes him away. "Okay," he says. But he doesn't seem okay.

We both keep eating, trying not to stare at Mom, both of us rooting for her to get the food to her mouth. It's like when we used to hike and we'd be three-quarters of the way to the end and Mom would yell, "We can do this!" and raise her arms in the air.

Maybe I should stand up, pump a fist in the air, and yell, "You can eat the spaghetti! You can do this!"

Mom gives it one more try, but her hands are trembling a little now. Dad helps her again, but she drops the fork and leans back in her chair.

"I'll make you some crackers," I tell her. "I'll put cheese on them, too. Okay?"

"That's a good idea," Dad says. He goes to the cupboard to get the Ritz box.

Mom sips her root beer and starts picking up the noodles with her fingertips, one at a time. She holds the noodle over her mouth and drops it in.

"That will work," I say, and I leave the Easy Cheese on the counter.

Mom eats the rest of her spaghetti with her fingers, red sauce gathering at the corners of her mouth. She looks straight at Dad, then at me, and says, "I think we need to go to the ocean tomorrow."

"We'll go soon," Dad says.

We'll go soon is the same as Dad saying, "Never."

"I swam with dolphins one time," Mom says.

Sometimes the disease makes her say outrageous things, like her past, present, and dreams get all mixed up together. "You did?"

Dad nods. "It's true, actually. She did."

"It was amazing." She has a faraway look in her eyes.

"There was a pod of dolphins just off the shore," Dad says, taking his plate to the sink, "and your mom was swimming there, too, and she got caught in the middle."

"I wish that could happen again." Mom licks the spaghetti sauce off her fork.

"Weren't you scared?"

"No, because I heard them talking and knew they were dolphins." Mom gives her plate to Dad. "They were too fast for me to keep up with them, though. I tried."

"It's good you couldn't keep up," Dad says. "You would've kept swimming!"

"I think I might have."

After Dad and I finish cleaning up, I go to my room and search for more pieces of dolphin that fit together.

I open the bottle of Gorilla Glue. Ever since Mom has been sick, I've had this dream where I'm surrounded by bottles of different kinds of glue. Mom sits in front of me, and I look into her brain with a Q-tip squeezed between my fingers. I dip the Q-tip in one of the bottles, using the glue to bond her memories together, trying to make them stick.

On the floor next to my bed is my sketchbook. I draw a detailed sketch of Mom's face, but the rest of her is dolphin. I use scissors to cut out the figure, dot the back with Elmer's glue, and step up on my desk. I press the sketch against the ocean poster, in the underwater space. Mom—part herself, part dolphin—is swimming among the other creatures of the ocean.

There's something missing, though. I cut three different size circles from the sketch paper and write "Cassie" inside them. I glue them on the poster between Dolphin Mom and the surface of the water, my name like bread crumbs, a path leading home.

THE BUCKET LIST

Usually on Sundays, Mom and Dad spend most of the morning in the kitchen, eating breakfast, drinking coffee, and reading, but not today. On the table are empty plates with leftover syrup and half-filled mugs, and instead of the clanking of forks against dishes, there's only the sound of rain falling on the back-porch roof.

Mom left a note on the counter. *"Good morning, Cassie. There are two BIG chocolate chip pancakes in the toaster oven. Dad and I went for a walk. We'll be back soon. Love you, Mom."*

Of course they went for a walk. It's raining, and Mom loves the rain. Out the window, drops are falling hard, some catching the light's reflection on the way down. Mom and Dad are probably wearing their matching plum rain jackets and not carrying an umbrella. Mom doesn't believe in owning one. *Cassie, you know I don't like to push my opinions on you—I want to give you space to form your own—except for how I feel about umbrellas. They're unnecessary.*

Umbrellas are unnecessary, but only if you have a good raincoat.

By the time I spread butter and pour syrup on my pancakes, there's lightning and thunder and it's raining so hard, drops are bouncing up off the ground.

I hear Mom outside. "Woo-hoo!"

The front door opens, and Dad takes off his raincoat before coming in. Lightning flashes, the house lights flicker, and Mom yells, "Amazing!"

"Is she going to stay out there?" I ask Dad.

"Maybe, just till the lightning passes."

"Cassie!" she calls to me. I peek out the door. She's leaning against the front porch railing. "Come out here with me."

In the distance, lightning cracks against the sky. Mom counts, "One thousand one, one thousand two . . ." She gets to twelve, and there's the sound of thunder, deep and loud. "The storm is a little more than two miles away."

She stares down at the ground, watching raindrops bounce and ping. "You know, when I was younger, after a hard rain, a big puddle used to form in front of my house. I can remember going out there and looking for worms. But I also used to imagine what it would be like to be small enough so the puddle would look like a giant lake, and I'd be able to dive in and swim across it."

"There're lots of real lakes you can swim across," I say.

Mom's quiet, and she keeps her eyes focused on the ground, on the raindrops. It's the kind of look she gets when she's analyzing data for her job. She's an accountant. She breaks down and organizes information, usually having to do with numbers. Calculating, according to her, is what she does best in the world. "Calculating and swimming."

"Yeah, there are lots of lakes," she says. "I don't know why I never swam any."

"You were busy doing other things?" I answer. "It happens."

She laughs. and it's funny that I'm the one being philosophical about life. "You're kind of smart." She kisses me on the forehead. "Aren't you?"

"I am."

The lightning has moved farther away. It's fifteen seconds before we hear thunder. "Okay, Mom, I'm going to get philosophical again," I say.

"I'm ready." Mom gives me a serious "thinking" look.

"Storms are kind of amazing. I mean, they're normal in the sense that we expect to see them this time of year, but for storms to happen, there have to be exact right conditions. It makes them unique."

"That's true," Mom says. "Our lives are like that, too, except—now *I'm* going to get philosophical—sometimes we can't wait for the right conditions to make our lives unique.

You just have to plan anyway, move forward, and see what happens."

We stay out on the porch until there's no more thunder.

Without taking off her jacket, Mom goes into the house. She seems to be on some sort of secret mission. She heads to the office and shuts the door, a sign Dad and I shouldn't disturb her.

I sit down in the living room, where Dad's reading a newspaper. "Did Mom talk about swimming in lakes when you were on your walk?"

"Kind of," he says from behind the paper. "We talked about where we want to go on our next vacation. She said she wanted to go to a place where there was good swimming. Ocean, lake, swimming pool. She wasn't particular."

He drops the paper to his lap. "What about you? Where'd you like to go?"

"Someplace we haven't been before." I shrug. "Or maybe a place where there are roller coasters."

"Okay," Dad says. "Good swimming and a roller coaster. Guess I'll find a place that has both."

"What about you?" I ask.

"Ice cream," he says. "That will be my contribution to our search. Good ice cream."

My sketch pad is on the coffee table. I open it to a blank page. I start by drawing roller-coaster tracks and then cars, falling down a steep drop. Instead of people riding in the cars, I draw scoops of ice cream for heads and cake and sugar cones for bodies. I use my colored pencils and draw candy sprinkles to outline arms, waving in the air.

In the foreground, at the bottom of the paper, I draw a mud puddle half the length of the roller coaster. At the edge of the puddle is another ice-cream cone, its rainbow-sprinkled arms positioned like it's getting ready to dive.

I color in the rest of the drawing, using shades that remind me of cotton candy, deep-fried Twinkies, glazed doughnuts, and blue summer skies.

The office door opens, and Mom comes into the living room, setting lime-green stationery on the coffee table. "Honey," she says to Dad, and pats the spot next to her on the couch.

She sits between us. "This," she says, "is my bucket list. In the next ten years, I want to have every place crossed off. I don't see any reason why that isn't possible."

She points at the first item on the list, which reads *"Swimming the English Channel"* and is followed by bullet points labeled *"Me," "John,"* and *"Cassie,"* each followed by details on how we can help. "I was serious about that one. I have a plan."

"I'm in," I say.

Dad leans forward. "Me too."

5

This morning, I sit outside the classroom door and work on sketching my idea for the ocean mural to present to Art Club.

A backpack lands against the classroom wall not far from where I'm sitting. It's red and black and has a couple of soccer patches sewn on it. I know it belongs to Bailey.

"Hi." I keep sketching.

"Hey." Bailey turns toward the soccer field, away from me.

"Come up with any more ideas for the mural?"

"Still thinking."

"How's your grandma?" I ask. "I miss seeing her. Tell her I say hi."

"I'll tell her." Bailey walks over to the fifth-grade equipment cart, but it's empty. She turns back to me. "You could tell her yourself, you know?"

I stop sketching and look over my book, toward the playground. Three kids hang upside down from the bars, and another stuffs a Rice Krispies Treat into his mouth, throws away the wrapper, and runs to the basketball court. A different group starts a four-square game.

"I'm sorry about your mom, Cassie, I really am, but . . . how long . . . ?" Bailey shakes her head. "I'm going to go play."

But how long . . . ?

Are you going to spend recesses alone?
Will it be before you feel like playing soccer again?
Will it be till our friendship goes back to normal?

———

In the classroom, right after announcements, Mrs. G says, "I'm going to let you work in pairs. But I will be choosing your partner."

I don't like when Mrs. G chooses our partners for us. I can work a lot faster by myself.

She starts pulling Popsicle sticks and announcing names. "Gavin and Emma. Jonathan and Celina. Joseph and Ava. Cassie and . . ." She looks up. Sean is raising his hand. "You have a question?"

"Can we work at the table?"

"Yes, but no more than two groups over there, please."

She goes back to calling out names. "Cassie and," she says again, "Bailey."

I don't look up. I doubt Bailey does, either.

Mrs. G finishes, and everyone gets into their groups. Everyone but Bailey and me. Neither of us gets up from our desk. I take a chance and start doing my math until Mrs. G notices I'm not working with a partner.

I get through the problems in the first section and four problems in the second; then I feel Mrs. G standing behind me. "You've decided to work alone, Cassie?"

Since the answer is obvious, I might as well admit it. "Yes. I . . ." But I can't think of any good way to complete my sentence.

"Bailey's your partner, right? One of you needs to sit next to the other, please."

I finally look up at Bailey. Her head is leaning against her hand, and she's holding the end of a pencil against her math book, but the pencil isn't moving. I'm pretty sure she can hear what Mrs. G is saying. I don't get up right away, waiting for her to make a move, but the only one she makes is to slouch in her chair.

I drag my math book off my desk, stepping around groups that are working on the floor. "What number are you on?"

At the top of her problem set, she's sketched a face of a

wolf, her favorite animal. "I'm on number one," she says. "And my grandma's doing fine."

But then she turns away from me again, sliding her book to the other side of her desk.

"Mrs. G wants us to work together." It used to be so easy to talk to Bailey, about soccer, about art, about why Takis are the best snack in the world.

"We can pretend to do that," she says. "That way you can still work by yourself. It's the way things are now, right? I've gotten used to it."

I want to tell her that when my mom got sick, it felt like I was swimming in the endless ocean. That there's a deep, wide-open space all around me, and I can't help but think about it all the time, even when I'm doing math, because breaking down numbers reminds me of pieces—of sand dollars, of glass dolphins, of letters that spell my name.

I want to tell her, "You don't understand. I'm helping my dad take care of my mom. She's everything, and I'm just trying to keep swimming."

I finish the first page and turn to the next. Mrs. G walks up behind us. "How are you two doing?" she asks.

"Good," Bailey and I say in unison.

She moves on to check in with the next group. I lean toward Bailey and whisper, "How are you really doing? We probably should work together a little."

"It's too late," Bailey says, pointing her pencil at Mrs. G, who's picking up the handle of her singing bowl.

"Okay, ladies and gentlemen," Mrs. G says. "Everyone back to your desks, and let's go over the math." I grab my pencil and my book. Sitting down at my own desk, I turn back to the first page.

Mrs. G picks up the container of Popsicle sticks. "Gavin, will you explain the first problem for us?" Gavin walks to the front of the room.

I glance up at Bailey. I remember the first time my mom and dad met her grandma. It was open house. We were in second grade, and they were eating the pizza the Parent Teacher Club was selling at the picnic tables while Bailey and I played soccer on the field. On the way home, my parents thought they were talking softly enough so I couldn't hear them over the music playing on the radio, but I heard just enough to figure out that Bailey's mom had been sick (the kind of sick that destroys your body, not your brain), and now her grandma took care of her sister and her.

I wanted to ask so many questions, but I decided to let Bailey bring it up herself. She did, once. Kind of. It was just a couple of years ago, during a soccer game. She'd scored a goal from midfield, and when everyone was finished giving her high fives, we ran to the sidelines together and she said, "My mom would've loved to see that."

Now I think about how my mom used to love to hear about math lessons. But she isn't the same mom anymore.

"Thank you, Gavin," Mrs. G says. I wasn't paying attention, but I check my answer, and it matches his. Mrs. G pulls another stick.

"Bailey," she says.

Bailey stares at her book. The classroom is quiet. Mrs. G usually gives us a little time to get our thoughts together when she calls on us to answer a question.

Everyone's looking at her, waiting. Over my shoulder, the clock reads nine thirty. Still fifteen minutes. Too much time left to be saved by recess.

"I don't know," Bailey says. "I don't have an answer."

"Cassie, how about you?" Mrs. G asks.

I could sit at my desk and pretend I didn't do the math, either. I could shake my head and repeat the words Bailey said: *I don't know. I don't have an answer.*

But I don't. I place my math sheet under the projector and share, "The dividend is 3.28, which I can also think about like thirty-two tenths and eight hundredths. The divisor is four, which goes into thirty-two eight times, and eight two times, giving me a quotient of eighty-two hundredths, which is 0.82."

"Good job, Cassie. Thank you." Mrs. G leans over

toward me and whispers, "But next time, you need to do your best to work with Bailey."

I nod.

———⬤

At recess, I find my usual spot on the bench, open my bag of Takis, and turn to a blank page in my sketchbook. As I set it on my lap and press down the pencil, I see red tennis shoes.

Bailey's eating chili lime Takis, too, cradling the purple bag in front of her. She's not happy. "That was embarrassing."

"I'm sorry."

Her three new friends, Nathan, Marissa, and Diana, stand by a tree, only a few feet away from us, as if they need to protect her.

"But it's my own fault," Bailey says. "I know how much you like working alone now."

After we found out my mom was sick, Bailey kept calling me. She'd call a couple of times a day, in the morning and at night, but I wouldn't call her back.

"I'm sorry . . . ," I say. *For everything.*

"Yeah, you keep saying that, Cassie."

"I do, don't I." I know it's not enough.

But it will have to be for today. "Bailey!" Diana kicks over a soccer ball, and they run out to the field.

I open my sketchbook to the page where I'd sketched my idea for drawing the mural. In the middle of the ocean, I add a soccer ball with eight legs stretching out from the patches.

I pour the rest of the chips in my mouth. I didn't mean to push Bailey away. It just happened. I couldn't think about anything but my mom. There wasn't space for her and me and our Saturdays filled with riding bikes and soccer.

I draw a horizon line. Maybe I can draw a sky, a dusk sky, filled with warm colors and a piece of the sun, red, the same shade as Bailey's tennis shoes.

6

It's Saturday morning, and I'm crunching on cinnamon toast and Mom's sipping coffee, sitting at her place by the window. It's cloudy, and the mountains aren't visible at all, but the sagebrush and dirt are still there with their deep greens and reds. It is beautiful, all the space.

Some Saturdays, Dad has to work. Today is one of those days. He pours himself some coffee, too, and kisses Mom on the cheek.

"Would it be okay if Mom and me went on a bike ride?" I ask.

"Mom can't ride a bike. I mean, she could, but she might take off, and it would be hard to stop her."

"What if she sat on my bike seat, and I pedaled her around?"

"Maybe you can think of something else to do." Dad

washes out his mug. "Why don't you start your oil paint-ing? Mom can be your model again."

I'd rather ride my bike. "Yeah, I don't know. I'll think about it."

Dad grabs his lunch from the counter. "Be home around two."

I try something else. "Can we go for a walk? I won't take her far. She was fine on our walk the other day."

"What if she sits down on the curb and doesn't want to move?" I think Dad feels like if he gives me these what-if scenarios, he'll talk me out of going.

"Well, I'll just sit down next to her and wait."

"What if she starts—"

"I'll tell you exactly the route we're going to take, and I'll call you when we get back to the house."

Dad unhooks his keys from the key rack. "Just call me in an hour, okay?"

"We'll probably be back before then."

"Be careful."

"We will." *Don't worry so much.*

I get dressed and grab my sketchbook. Before we leave, I help Mom put on her jacket.

"I don't need this," she says.

"You can take it off if you get hot."

She takes it off anyway. "I don't want it."

No jacket, then.

She and I walk side by side. She doesn't shuffle her feet like she does across the floor at home, and her eyes are on the sky, a cloudy sky that's decorated today with white and dark-gray clouds and a sliver of blue peeking through to the north, just above the summit, belonging to a mountain she's hiked a hundred times.

We stop where the road meets the desert. I reach for beach chairs we've hidden behind some sagebrush. I start to unfold them, but Mom keeps walking.

Dad would tell me to get her back to the road. "Take her arm and lead her back. She could fall."

She's fine, Dad. I'll walk with her. She'll be okay.

Mom stops and reaches up to the clouds. From here, they do look close enough to touch, just like the mountains. The wide-open space makes things look smaller.

Red Dirt Canyon is in front of us. I reach up and caress Mom's elbow. "Let's stop here." I don't want her to get too close to the edge.

"No," she says and keeps walking. "There's the canyon!" She seems surprised. Maybe she forgot about it, too.

She must see I look worried. "I'm not going to fall into it. Don't worry."

The canyon rocks are shades of red and green, just like the desert floor. We stand close enough so we see about a quarter of the way down on the other side.

Mom sits, takes off her shoes, and turns around, waving for me to follow. I take off my shoes, too, and we scoot forward together, letting our sock-covered feet wiggle over the canyon edge.

The only sound is the wind. Mom lies down and closes her eyes.

"Your dad's not home," she says, "so we don't have to worry about going back. You should lie down, too. It's nice."

I do. I lie down and close my eyes and see light and the shadows of clouds. "What do you see when you close your eyes?"

I wonder if what she sees now is different from what she used to see. Before, she probably saw a sky filled with kites, a beach, or us dancing in a parking lot to Cyndi Lauper.

"Right now," she says, "I don't see anything. I'm just listening to the wind. What do you see?"

"I think about stuff more than I see images."

"Like what?"

"I think about school and about Dad and about you."

"Don't think too much," she says. "It's not every day

you get to be this close to the edge of a beautiful canyon and just listen to the wind."

"It feels like we're at the end of the earth."

"Yes, it does. I love it."

"More than the ocean?"

"Almost."

I tug on her elbow and have to see her, to remind myself she's still there. Mom lets me. Somehow, she knows.

There are times like these when I have to stop myself from thinking Mom is all of a sudden getting better. I wait for her to say something else, hoping it's my name. Her eyes hold mine for a few seconds and then focus over my shoulder, back to the mountains.

Mom finds my hand and threads her fingers with mine. "I love you . . ." She pauses, and I know she's searching for my name. *I love you, Cassie.*

"I love you, too," I tell her.

I take her advice and focus on listening to the wind, but then she starts humming "Girls Just Want to Have Fun," and it's better than that. It's a better feeling than being at the edge of the earth.

I hum the line about wanting to walk in the sun, and drift in the sound of Mom and her favorite song, so much that I fall asleep.

The wind is stronger now. Opening my eyes, I feel sand blow across my feet. I look over, and she's gone. "Mom!"

A trail of footprints leads in the opposite direction from the canyon. In the distance, I see her and let out a breath. She's sitting in one of the beach chairs I set up. She waves.

Dad can never know about this. I'd never hear the end of the "what ifs." "What if she had fallen off the edge of the canyon?" "What if she'd just walked away and we had to call the police to find her?"

I was supposed to call him. I grab my phone from my back pocket, the one Dad bought for me when Mom got sick. He's called three times. One right after the other, his first call forty-five minutes ago. I don't bother listening to the messages he left. The service is bad out here anyway. I'll call him when we get home.

I slip my feet inside my shoes and help Mom get on hers.

Dad's sitting on the porch steps when we get back. "Where have you been?" He's not happy.

"We were out for a walk," I tell him. "I thought you were at work?"

"You didn't call me back."

Mom walks past me. There's red dirt on the back of her sweater and pants. I forgot to brush her off.

"I tried to call, but the service was bad . . ." I can't tell him we were out by the canyon. "You came home because I didn't call?"

"I was worried, Cassie. Whenever I call, you're supposed to . . ." He's trying to control his voice, but it's shaky, like he wants to shout.

"I tried . . ." I brush the dirt off Mom's back. She elbows me. She doesn't want me brushing her.

"What are you doing, Cassie?" Dad sees her elbow me again.

"Mom got a little dirt on her back."

He comes around and looks. "That's more than *a little*. What happened? Did she fall?"

"No." I'm going to tell him the truth. "She wanted to lie down on the ground."

"Why?"

"Because she wanted to. Because she's Mom."

Dad brushes the dirt off the back of her pants. "I told you . . ."

"Nobody got hurt."

"Don't let her do that next time, okay?"

"Why not? It was one of the best times we've had. She was happy. I was happy." I hope Dad can hear my frustration. I'm not trying to be disrespectful. I really want to know why exactly he doesn't want Mom to lie down on the dirt.

"Just don't let her do it again."

As Dad takes Mom into the house, he asks her, "Where did you go?"

"We went to listen to the wind."

"And where did you go listen to the wind?"

I hold my breath. *Don't say we went to the canyon.* But she says something I'm not sure is better or worse. "You know what I'd really like to hear? The sound of dolphins in the wild again." She glances back at me and waves.

I'd forgotten about her bucket list. When I get inside the house, I head straight to the office. The paper she wrote on was lime-green stationery. It shouldn't be hard to find. The top drawer is filled with pencils, pens, and a box of staples. The middle drawer is filled with paper. I dig through the stack, but there's not a shade of green.

She does have a drawer in her nightstand next to her bed. I tiptoe to Mom and Dad's bedroom and open the drawer. The paper is right on top. The list of places is on the first page:

1. Swim the English Channel
2. Swim with dolphins (again, for longer this time)
3. Visit Machu Picchu
4. Visit the Louvre with Cassie
5. See the northern lights

I don't think Mom should need to give up all her dreams.

The English Channel, Machu Picchu, and the Louvre would take getting on a plane with a passport and would cost too much money. I've been saving some money to go to the Georgia O'Keeffe Museum in Santa Fe, but I don't have enough for probably even one plane ticket to Peru or to France. I remember she told us you could see the northern lights in Alaska, Greenland, or Iceland, but all those places are far, too.

But swimming with dolphins is possible.

7

Right when I get into class, I grab a Chromebook. I set a book on my desk to make it look like I'm taking a reading test.

During announcements, I google "places to swim with dolphins near Arizona," but then Mrs. G walks up to the front of the class, passing behind me. I close my Chromebook.

"How'd you do on your test?" Mrs. G asks.

I'm almost caught. "Uh . . . actually, there wasn't a test for the book I read."

"Let me see the title?"

I give Mrs. G the book. "Hmm, there definitely should be a test for *The Unteachables*. I'll help you look later."

"Thanks, Mrs. G." I better find some time today to finish reading the book.

"Good morning," she turns and says to the class. "Please get out your math journals and math books."

I like Mrs. G for a lot of reasons, but the biggest one is that she loves math.

"Today," she says, "we're going to continue our journey into decimals and fractions. Now, you all know how much I love dividing decimals . . ."

She claps her hands and rubs them together, like a magician right before performing a trick. She does this when she's excited about sharing something with us. "Okay, everyone, get out your place value charts. I'm going to give us a chance to perform some magic."

She twirls around and grabs a pen. "I've mentioned this before, but what makes decimals so amazing is that they allow us to break down a number to the minutest—the smallest, most microscopic—value."

She writes "0.000000000001" on the board. "That number is one trillionth. I can continue placing zeros in front of the one and keep going until the end of time." She writes another number on the board. "And some numbers are irrational—like two divided by three equals 0.6666666 . . . They go on and on and on." She holds the pen up in the air like it's a wand. "It's incredible to think about something going on forever."

Henry raises his hand. "What does *irrational* mean?" he asks.

I know what "irrational" *usually* means. When the doctor was talking to Dad and me about Mom right when she got diagnosed, he said there was a chance that she would show "irrational" behavior.

I raise my hand this time.

"Yes, Cassie."

"Well, I think irrational means something that doesn't follow the rules."

"Very good." I guess I'm on the right track.

Mrs. G takes us through the lesson, and we work on example problems, decomposing numbers in our math journals. I think about Mom.

I imagine that if I could decompose memories to the minutest images, maybe these tiny bits would have a chance to squeeze through the tiniest openings in the fatty tissue of her brain and at least give Mom the chance to see a part of them. Like, maybe she won't be able to remember everything about the Christmas she and Dad gave me my first bike, but she might be able to remember the color of the bike. It was blue.

When we get to our problem sets, Mrs. G says that today we can either choose our own partners or work by ourselves.

I open my math book. Across the room, Bailey gets out of her seat and sits at the desk next to Emma's.

It doesn't take long for me to finish my work. When we complete a task, we're supposed to do practice lessons. I take the Chromebook out of my desk and click the link, but I open a search window, too.

I get out *The Unteachables* just in case and stare over the edge, toward the screen. Sliding my hand under it, I type, "Swimming with dolphins Southern California." I push the Enter key.

The Zen singing bowl rings. "Ten more minutes," Mrs. G says.

She makes her way over to me. "Let's see if we can find that test."

She types in the book title and finds it right away.

"Thanks," I say. I take the test, guessing the answers for the last five questions, and then try my Google search again.

The closest place is in San Diego, about a three-hour drive from here.

Three hours is not that far. We could go on a Saturday, or during spring break. It would be worth the drive even if Mom did act "irrationally" once we got there.

I type, "Bus schedule to San Diego, California." There are lots of options. If Dad doesn't go along with my idea, my problem will be getting Mom to the bus station.

Staring at all the different departing and arriving times

makes me nervous; then being nervous turns into that heavy feeling I've gotten used to carrying around with me.

Mrs. G grabs her container of Popsicle sticks. I put my screen down.

She pulls a name. "Bailey, would you like to explain number one?"

The room is quiet, just like the other day. Bailey slouches down in her chair, too, and leans over her book. She'll wait out the quiet even though everyone's staring at her. And this morning, Mrs. G is giving her an extra-long time to answer. But I know Bailey, and the look on her face means she doesn't have one.

The longer the quiet lasts, the more I feel like I should help her. I kind of owe it to her.

"So." I speak up without raising my hand. "The problem is thirty-two divided by one hundred and ninety-six." I don't pause, because if I do, Mrs. G might say something about how it's not my turn. "So the number thirty-two is the dividend, how much you have altogether. We're going to take it and divide it into one hundred and ninety-six parts, our divisor. Our quotient would be the value of one of those parts."

When I'm finished, the classroom is still quiet, and Bailey is slouched farther down into her chair. She doesn't seem relieved.

"Very good, Cassie," Mrs. G says, "but next time, please raise your hand."

She looks up at the clock. "We'll go over the rest when we come in from recess."

As I stand up to get my snack out of my backpack, Bailey's still sitting at her desk, staring at me with her Wonder Woman / Joan of Arc look.

Soon as I get to the bench and open my bag of Takis, she stands in front of me. "You didn't have to help me. Please don't do that again."

I can't seem to do things right around her, not anymore.

She heads out to the soccer field.

"Fine, I won't do it again!" I yell.

"Good!" Bailey yells back. She dribbles the ball to get in line to be picked for a soccer team. So I get in line, too.

"You're going to play?" she asks so everyone can hear.

"Yeah, I'm going to play."

"Your skills are probably rusty."

"Guess we'll see, right?"

Bailey and I are on opposite teams.

I need her to see that I can still play, that not everything has changed. The game starts, and she takes the ball. I don't let her have any room to pass. My eyes focus on her feet.

She kicks the ball around me, into my team's half of the field, and I run to try and beat her to it. I stick out my foot to kick it and accidentally trip her.

I don't stop playing. I pass the ball downfield to one of my teammates. Running inside the penalty area, I set up for an instep kick, but Bailey's bumping my shoulder, our feet tangled up with the ball. We both fight for it.

Bailey kicks it loose, and I chase after her. One of the boys on her team waves his arms in the air and yells, "I'm open. Over here!"

But Bailey dribbles the ball all the way down. She takes a shot, but my foot gets there just in time to block it.

We both run after the ball, and even though the bell rings and everyone else goes to line up, Bailey and I keep playing.

I steal the ball. Bailey steals it back from me.

A whistle blows. "Girls!" It's Ms. Shelley, one of the yard duty ladies. "The bell rang! Let's get in line, please!"

"We need to finish this game," Bailey yells back.

Both of us keep moving. It feels good to play soccer with Bailey again, and it feels really good to run and kick the ball as hard as I can.

We're on the opposite end of the field when I hear Ms. Shelley's walkie-talkie, but I have to keep focused on the ball, on Bailey's footwork, on keeping my balance when she nudges into me.

I slide my foot under the ball, flip it up, and run out ahead of Bailey in the wide-open field. But she catches up to me and taps the back of my foot with hers, and I fall to the ground. I get up fast and run toward her, pushing her shoulder. She pushes back. Both of us fight for the ball, ignoring everything else around us.

I look up toward the goal. I don't know how much time has passed since the bell rang, but the playground is empty except for Bailey and me, and Mrs. Jones, our vice principal. She's standing next to the goal. Her arms are folded across her chest, and she has a you've-earned-detention look on her face.

8

On our way home in the car, I wait for Dad to say something about getting a call from Mrs. Jones, but he doesn't. Maybe he's waiting for me to mention it, or maybe my getting in trouble is not even on his mind.

"I have to spend time in detention at recess tomorrow."

He looks in the rearview mirror. "What happened?"

"Thought Mrs. Jones would've called you."

"She did."

"So you already know what happened with Bailey and me."

Dad nods. "I wanted to hear your side of the story."

"We were playing soccer, and we wanted to finish the game. It felt good to play soccer with . . . It won't happen again."

"I haven't seen Bailey in a long time. How's she doing?"

I shrug and turn toward the window. "Okay, I guess."

Dad seems like he wants to say something, but he lets it go.

When we get home, there's knocking coming from the hallway.

"Kimberly," Mrs. Collins is saying, "please open the door."

Dad and I freeze and watch Mrs. Collins come into the living room, then move into the kitchen, without noticing us. A drawer opens, and there's the sound of rustling spoons, forks, knives. That, or Mrs. Collins has opened the junk drawer and is searching through who-knows-what.

She comes out carrying a screwdriver, rushing straight down the hallway. I hear the jiggling of a doorknob.

Dad throws down his lunch pail and coat. "Mrs. Collins?"

The jiggling stops. "Oh, Mr. Rodrigues, I'm so sorry. Kimberly has locked herself in the bathroom, and she won't open the door. She was taking a bath, and . . ."

Dad uses the screwdriver to unlock the door. "Kim . . ."

Mom's sitting in the bathtub, her legs folded against her chest, chin resting on her knees.

"Kim." Dad grabs a towel. "Come on—it's time to get out."

But Mom doesn't move. "I want to stay here."

Dad scoops the water to check the temperature. "It's getting cold."

"I want to stay here," Mom says again.

I wait for Dad to do something. He always does. He fixes things or cleans up messes. He's always able to convince Mom. But not this time. He looks up at Mrs. Collins. Then at me.

"Mrs. Collins, you can go ahead and go," he says. "Thank you. Cassie, we'll take turns sitting here with Mom, okay?"

"She's going to get too cold," I say. I step inside the bathroom and check the water myself. "Can't you lift her out? Dad . . ."

His hands are covering his face. He's crying.

"Dad, it's okay. I'll help you."

I give him a second. He drops his hands and rests them on his hips, then wraps his arms around me. "It's going to be okay?"

Dad says it like a question. I don't know what else to say but, "Yeah, we're going to be all right."

He pats me on the shoulder and turns to Mom, back to being the grown-up. "Kim, can you stand up?"

Mom doesn't move.

"Cassie and I are going to lift you out of the tub," he says. "You have to be getting cold."

Dad slips his hand under Mom's arms. As he lifts Mom to her feet, water splashing, I wonder if she's been preparing herself, building her tolerance for cold water.

"The water in the English Channel is around fifty-eight to sixty-five degrees," she told me once, "depending on the season, so it's better if you get your body acclimated first. But it's also important to pay attention to the currents. They're strong and can push you to the side, off course, and you could spend hours swimming and not moving forward at all. In those conditions, it's a little hard to find your way across."

I hold out my hands to help her step out of the bathtub. Dad wraps the towel around Mom and kisses her on the cheek. There are tears still in his eyes. "Let's go get dressed," he says.

I don't want to cry.

I'm tired of feeling sad.

I don't want to think about Mom fading away.

She always told me to not let my sadness dictate my actions. "You can definitely be sad," she said, "but try to keep moving." Like the Albert Einstein quote in our classroom.

I know Mom's own dad died when she was seven

years old. Swimming, she said, was a way to keep moving forward. It was her way of keeping sadness from weighing her down.

———————

I sit at my desk and find pieces of dolphin that match. I've put together six, and the bowl is still full. Two out of the six have different color flukes, a green fluke with blue pectoral fins and head, a pink fluke with a red-pink body and blue head. They're whole, though, and that's what matters.

Hanging on the wall above my bed is a framed photograph of Mom and me. We're standing by a sign, OVERLOOK TRAIL—10.4 MILES. Both of us have our arms up in the air, flexing them to show our muscles, with serious, determined looks on our faces.

I take down the frame, unhook the back, and slide out the photograph. Walking to the extra bedroom, I use the scanner on the printer to make a copy.

Back in my bedroom, I grab scissors and glue and take my sketchpad out of my backpack.

Staring at the photograph, I think about that number Mrs. G wrote on the board, 0. 000000000001.

If this picture of Mom and me were a math problem and I had to explain my strategy for cutting it into pieces,

I'd say this: maybe my mom can't recognize the whole picture, but she might be able to recognize one part of it. She might remember what color socks she wore, or how it started to rain, or how the shoestring on one of my hiking boots kept coming untied.

I have to remind myself that breaking down a memory doesn't mean she's going to remember any of it.

But I have to try.

I start with me. I cut around my arms, and my fists, and glue it to a page in my notebook.

Under the picture, I write, *"This is Cassie."* I do the same with the picture of my mom and glue it to a different part of the page. Under it, I write, *"This is you."* The last part of the photograph I cut out is the sign. I glue it to another part of the page and write, *"We had just finished a hike."*

The parts of the photograph tell a simple story. I was there. My mom was there. We went on a hike.

One photo divided by three parts. I scribble the equation. Three goes into one zero times; then three goes into ten three times, and it keeps repeating. 3.33333333 . . .

It's an irrational number, the kind that goes on forever. I like that. I call the photo collage *0.3333333*. It makes sense that the three parts of my mom, me, and something we did together have a value that is endless.

In the living room, Mom is now dressed, her hair still wet. Dad's making dinner. On the television, the camera shows a close-up of a dolphin's eye, then zooms out, farther and farther, so that the image is a pod of at least fifty or so dolphins swimming in the open ocean that goes on for miles and miles. Dad put on her favorite DVD to calm her down.

"Are they going somewhere?" They look like they're swimming with purpose.

"They're just swimming," Mom says. My question brings her out of her trance. "That's what they do."

I hold my sketchbook in front of her and point to the piece of photograph that shows just the sign. "We used to go hiking a lot."

Mom points at the photograph, too, and rubs it with her fingers. Then she slides her fingers over to the next piece, a pair of untied shoelaces.

"Those hiking boots I wore always came untied," I tell her.

Mom's fingers move up and down our faces, like she's trying to release them from the picture. "We loved to hike," she says. "We could hike forever. Like how I could swim forever."

I kiss her on the cheek. The photograph sparks something in her memory. Not enough to remember my name, but it was one photograph, only one decomposed memory, a piece that found its way.

———•

In the extra bedroom, there are shelves filled with trophies. They all belong to Mom. She really was a great swimmer. The butterfly was her best stroke.

Next to one of the trophies is a framed picture from when she was about nine or ten years old. She stands on top of a diving block holding another trophy. She has short, blond, almost-white hair that reflects the sun. Her smile is just as shiny.

On a bottom shelf, there are boxes filled with photographs Mom never framed. I take the lid off one of the boxes and sort the pictures by who's in them. One pile is just me, one pile is Mom and me, another pile is Mom and Dad, another pile is all three of us. There aren't many of just Dad and me.

Then I make a pile of the ones I think are the best. Where we look the happiest.

I choose ten to scan and spread the printouts on my bedroom floor.

The first one I start to cut was taken at a lake. Mom and I are in our bathing suits. Mom's wearing a hat, and I have zinc oxide on my nose.

I cut the sides off first, making my way to our faces. I cut around Mom's hat and around my head. Between us, I glue a piece with water and sand. The picture I create is just our faces, the water, and the ground under our feet.

The next photograph I cut into pieces is one of the three of us camping. Dad must've set a timer on the camera. He and Mom are sitting in beach chairs with their arms around each other, and I'm standing by Mom with my arms raised to the sky.

Before cutting, I look at the photograph hard and deep. I zero in on my smile. It's big and toothy. I can't remember the last time I smiled like that.

I pick up the photo of ten-, eleven-year-old Mom, standing on the diving block, holding the trophy. Everything about the picture is bright: her smile, her yellow shirt, her eyes, the future.

I have to find a way to get Dad to take us to San Diego.

Dad loves art as much as I do, so it might be a way to get him to change his mind. I have a piece of poster board in my closet. I have poster paint, too.

I sit on my bedroom floor. I'm going to keep it simple. Using the brightest color paint I have, I write "WISH WE WERE HERE." Then I draw a sketch of Mom and a dolphin, their heads breaching the surface of the water, Mom waving to Dad and me. We have our arms in the air, cheering for her. I add one big talking bubble above us. Inside I write, "WE MADE IT!"

When I'm finished, Dad's still in the kitchen making dinner, so I have a chance to hang the poster in the living room. Every once in a while, I catch him staring at the portrait of Mom I sketched last year. I tape the poster next to it.

I hope this doesn't make him mad, and now I think maybe I should go out and give him a heads-up about it.

I sit down next to Mom. My heart is beating fast, loud, interrupting the narrator on the documentary she's watching. I reach out to her hand, which is resting on the couch. I hold it. I squeeze it. She squeezes back. She won't take her eyes off the TV, but I rest my head on her shoulder, and she leans in to me, too.

This is why we should help her with the list. She's not a robot.

Behind the faraway eyes, Mom is still there. We shouldn't give up on that. We still have places to go.

"Do you know why dolphins swim in groups?" Mom asks, focusing on the TV screen.

"For protection?" I say.

"Yes, but did you know they can leave the group any-time they want? They can go join a different one. There's a lot of freedom in being able to do that. The other pods will protect the new dolphins, too."

Sometimes I think the best thing that could happen to Mom would be to turn into a dolphin. That one day we'd come home and Mrs. Collins would have had to move her to the bathtub to keep her safe. Then Dad would have to buy a giant tank and fill it with water. But it eventually wouldn't be big enough, so we'd have to drive her to the ocean.

We would carry Mom to the water's edge. She'd give us a click and nod her head up and down, her way of saying, "Goodbye. I love you." We'd give her an extra push into the water, and the waves would rock her back and forth. We'd watch her swim out, her dorsal fin visible from shore, and she'd lift her head one more time, give us another nod and click, and then disappear underwater, swimming out to the wide-open space. We'd miss her, but we'd know she was happy, that she was where she belonged.

If Mom did turn into a dolphin, there might be a chance she'd get her memory back.

Since dolphins can recognize sounds unique to others, right before she dived down into the water, I'd say "Cassie" one last time, and she would hear it. And one day, in fifteen, twenty, twenty-five years, I'd stand on the same beach, and I'd say my name out loud, thinking I'm just saying it for the ocean to hear, but maybe my mom, the dolphin, would breach the water's surface and whistle at me.

She'd have recognized my unique sound.

Soon as we sit down for dinner, I keep working on Dad. "You know how Mom really likes dolphins? Well, there are places people can go and pay to get in the water with them. I was thinking it would be a great thing to do for her. Maybe . . ."

I'm about to say, "Maybe it would bring some of her memory back . . ." but the idea wouldn't sound reasonable to Dad at all. He'd think it was impossible.

"I don't know, Cassie," he says. "I don't know how she would react once we got there or even how she would respond to the dolphins. It might put a lot of stress on her. None of us needs more stress."

But what if the opposite is true? That it doesn't bring us more stress, that seeing Mom with the dolphins, whether she's actually swimming with them or just standing in the water with one, will make us the happiest we've been in a while?

"Well, I can make the reservations." I pretend to ignore him. "And everything, if you don't want to be bothered by it. And I'll help you if anything happens. I'll even help pay for it. I've been saving money . . ."

"You've been saving money to go to the Georgia O'Keeffe Museum."

"So the museum can wait."

"I have work, and you have school," he says.

"We can go on a weekend."

"What if she walks off?" Dad starts the what-if game again. "What if she doesn't like something and gets mad? What if we're in public, and she starts throwing things?"

"Then you'll have me to help you. And what if we did go"—I'm going to play the what-if game, too—"and nothing happened? What if it turned out to be a normal trip? What if Mom loved it? What if we had one of the best times ever? And what if . . ."

I'm about to say, "It was the last time we got a chance to go anywhere all together?" but I don't. It wouldn't be fair to Dad.

"It's a good thought, Cassie. Your mom would love to swim with dolphins. I should've taken her before."

I'm glad he agrees it's a good idea, but I know it's one more way of saying no. "We can still have good times, you know?" I say.

"Maybe," he says. But the look on his face says, "This might be impossible, too."

I've never liked the word "maybe." That's why I like math. There's no "maybe." Math is precise. There might be different ways to get to an answer, but there's only one answer.

"I made something for us." I get up from the table and lead him into the living room. He follows me right away. He probably thinks he's going to see something I've done for the art show.

At first, Dad looks at the photos glued to the poster and has no real expression at all; then he smiles a little. But then his smile goes back to being a straight line, 180 degrees of "This is not a good idea."

He goes back to the kitchen to finish his dinner. "Cassie," he says, "I understand what you're doing, but I've made my decision. I'm sorry. I'm doing what I think is best for your mom. I know this is hard, and it's not going to get easier. This is our life now."

I know this is our life now, and it's hard. "But we don't have to make it harder," I say.

Dad just scrapes a fork against his plate.

You're wrong, I want to tell him. *You're afraid. There isn't any reason why we shouldn't be who we were before. We can at least try.*

After I clean the dishes, I take down the poster and hang it in my room. In my desk drawer, I find an envelope that I decorated with Georgia O'Keeffe flowers. I take out all the cash I've stashed in it and start counting.

9

It's first recess on Monday, and Bailey and I are serving detention. I'm on one side of the room, and she's on the other. We had to bring something to keep us busy while we were in here: for her, schoolwork and a book, and for me, my sketch pad.

There are only three other kids in the room with us. The one rule: no talking. The only sound is the opening of chip bags.

I start drawing my stick figures, and in front of one of them, I draw a soccer ball. A detailed one, where I shade in the spaces to show a checkered pattern. On both sides of the paper, I sketch goal nets and draw short, jagged lines for the grass to represent the field.

I set down my pencil and stretch my fingers. Across the room, Bailey's erasing something in her math book, then wiping the shavings onto the floor. She reaches for some Takis. From here, I can see her fingertips. They're stained red from the chili flavoring.

Mine are, too.

On one of the sketch figures I've drawn, I start to add details—a soccer jersey with the number seven, the number I always requested when I used to play, plus black shorts and cleats. I add features to the face; the person's eyes—I guess mine—are focused on the soccer ball.

For the second person, I don't start with a stick figure. I draw the way I used to, the way I drew Mom's portrait. I fill in details, writing the number three on the jersey.

I look around the room to see if there are colored pencils or crayons but don't spot any.

Ms. Debbie is the aide staying in here with us. I get up—I don't know if it's against the rules or not—and whisper, "Is there anything I can use to color?"

"Do you need them for something you have to finish for school?" she asks.

"Yes, it's something I have to finish."

"Okay, go back to where you were sitting, and I'll bring them to you." She goes to a corner of the room, finds a container of crayons, and sets them on my desk.

There's one broken red crayon with the paper peeled

off. I use it to color in the shoes and the jersey, except for the number.

In third grade, I remember telling Bailey that out of all the math operations, she was most like multiplication.

She thought that was a funny and weird thing to say. I thought it was the highest compliment I could give her.

"What do you mean by that?" she'd asked me.

It was an easy answer for me because I really believed it was true. I was prepared to support my answer with strong, solid reasons, even in third grade.

If I were to answer the question now, I'd have even more details.

Being like multiplication is a good thing. When you multiply whole numbers, the product is always greater than the numbers you started with. I kind of think of you like this: first, your courage, which is represented by what you do with your eyes—you always look directly at a person when you're speaking to them or when they're speaking to you, like you're doing now—that's the multiplicand. Your calmness is the multiplier. When you multiply those two factors together, you get a product that equals fierce.

I still feel that way about Bailey, but I'm not sure how she feels about me. I finish coloring the tip of one of the shoes, and then blow the crayon shavings off the picture.

The drawing is missing something. Talking bubbles.

I draw one next to the figure who's wearing the number seven. Inside I write, "I'm really sorry. I still think you're like multiplication." Then, underneath it, I write the equation $7 \times 3 = 21$. That was the number of goals Bailey and I always wanted to try and score in one game. The closest we came was eleven between the both of us.

Next to the figure with the number three jersey, I draw another bubble, but I don't know what to write. I could guess how Bailey would respond to my saying "I'm sorry" again, but it doesn't feel like I have a right to. That's for her to decide, so I draw a question mark.

I fold the paper in half and walk across the room, putting the container back where Ms. Debbie found it.

I hold the drawing down by my leg, and on the way back to where I was sitting, I pass Bailey's desk. I make sure Ms. Debbie isn't looking and set the paper next to Bailey's math book.

Back at my desk, I open to a blank page in my sketch pad, but I can't concentrate on drawing anything more.

Soon, we're dismissed. Bailey tucks her math book under her arm and leaves. On my way out, I notice the paper. It fell on the floor; I'm not sure if she accidentally dropped it or did it on purpose, but either way, I pick it up and slide it into my back pocket.

Later, while everyone else is packing up and leaving the classroom, Bailey and I stay. We have Art Club.

Mrs. G says she needs our help with something. We follow her down the hallway, toward the front of the school. "I'm very excited about this mural project. No matter what we paint, it's going to be beautiful, because we worked together to create it. And working together is a beautiful thing."

Right before the office is a door that says SUPPLY ROOM. Mrs. G opens it with a key. "I'm going to cut some paper and hand it to you. We can use it to plan out the mural."

Bailey and I stand in the hallway, and it's quiet. I feel like I should say something. "How's your grandma?" I ask again. I can't think of anything else.

"She's still doing good, but she's always doing good," Bailey says.

"She did always seem happy."

"Yep, that's her."

I want to ask Bailey exactly how old Grandma Lorena is. She has to be ten, fifteen, maybe twenty years older than my mom. *Does she still drive? If she does, does she at least forget where she puts her keys? Does she sometimes put crackers—Ritz, Saltines, Cheez-Its—in the refrigerator? Has she ever forgotten your name, just for a second?*

Mrs. G carries the roll of butcher paper, and we go back

to the classroom. The other Art Club members are waiting by the door.

"First thing we have to do is choose our theme." She points to the white board where she wrote down our choices. "Now, before we vote, if you have other ideas, I will add them as options. Does anyone have any?"

No one raises their hand.

"So it will either be the ocean or the desert, then. Are we ready to vote?" Mrs. G asks.

"No," I say. I grab my sketchbook. "Is it okay if I show something to the club?"

"Absolutely," Mrs. G replies.

"Can I use the projector so everyone can see?"

While Mrs. G turns on the projector, I open up the sketchbook to my ocean drawing. It's not completely finished, but it'll give the club an idea of what I have in mind.

I slide the drawing under the projector and move over to the SMART board. "So my idea is to have an ocean in the background, but I thought about how a lot of people wanted a desert theme, too . . ." I point to where I've drawn sagebrush, a roadrunner, some desert flowers, and a saguaro cactus floating through the waves. "So there's also a stingray," which is gliding around the cactus, "and different colored fish," which are swimming in and out of sagebrush, "and a dolphin," which is breaching the water, and instead of giving the illusion that it's jumping over the sun, it's leap-ing over a desert marigold. "And we can even add more desert things if people want."

The room is quiet. By the looks on everyone's faces, I have a feeling they don't like my idea of mixing the desert and ocean, of meeting halfway.

"Thank you, Cassie," Mrs. G says. "I'm going to add 'both' to our list of choices."

Jonathan raises his hand. "I'm not trying to be mean or anything, Mrs. G, but I still don't get what the ocean would mean to us? The mural is supposed to be for the whole school, and like I said before, it should connect to where we live—our community."

"Well, you're right, Jonathan, but it's always good to explore different ideas." Mrs. G is probably trying to pro-tect my feelings.

"Color," I speak up, interrupting her. "I guess I was thinking of the theme for the mural being more about color than things we drew. So"—I go back to the projector—"there would be a mix of warm and cool colors, you know, the sad and the happy."

"But," Bailey says, "we can mix the colors in the desert mural, too. I still think Jonathan's right about it connect-ing to us more. But I like the idea of making sure we use colors that represent different emotions." It's not what I expected her to say.

"Are we ready to vote, then?" Mrs. G asks.

Everyone says, "Yes," including me.

There's one vote for "both" and eleven votes for "desert."

"All right, we have our idea." Mrs. G walks by and pats me on the shoulder. "I'm going to put you in groups of two, give you each a piece of the butcher paper." She rolls the paper from the supply room across the classroom floor. "And I want you and your partner to draw a panel of your own creation. That way we can incorporate everyone's perspectives. Then we'll put them together to see what it looks like. Now, if you want, you can work on them here at school, or if it's okay with your parents, you can work on them at home." Mrs. G goes to her desk and holds up a stack of papers. "I have notes explaining the mural. I will also be sending an email, if any of your parents have questions."

My mom used to have questions about everything. But I'm not sure she even uses the computer anymore.

Mrs. G passes out a note to each of us. "Time to pick partners. I want you all to stand in a straight line, shoulder to shoulder, and count off."

Each person in the club is assigned a number, one through twelve. "Okay," Mrs. G says, "number one, you're partners with number twelve, number two with number eleven, number three with number ten . . ."

I'm number five. Bailey's number eight. We're partners again.

Bailey grabs a note from Mrs. G and a piece of butcher paper. "I'm on my bike, so can you keep the paper with you? We can work at my house this Saturday if you want?"

"I can't. My dad works this Saturday, and I have to stay home with my mom. Sorry."

Bailey leaves the paper on her desk. "I'll come over to your house, then. That okay?"

"It's okay. It's just, my mom . . . If you don't want to be partners, we can talk to Mrs. G."

"No." Bailey finds a key to what is probably her bike lock. "I'm fine with it." She slides her arms through her backpack. "See ya."

As I'm walking to the after-school program, Mrs. G calls me back to the classroom. "Just want to see if you're okay with the club's decision?"

"Yeah," I say, but even though I'm okay with it, that doesn't mean I'm not going to be thinking about how I can disguise a stingray within a jackrabbit or a dolphin in a saguaro cactus.

"You shouldn't be disappointed. You spoke up about your vision. That's a good thing. If you haven't started creating anything for the art show, maybe it could be something like what you described to the club?"

"Maybe. I don't know if it would work on a smaller scale. But I'll think about it."

———◆

By the bike rack, Bailey hasn't left yet. She stuffs her lock, chain, and key in a small pocket of her backpack and leans forward to get a look at the front tire. It's flat. She unzips a side pocket and takes out a small canvas pouch.

It doesn't take Bailey more than a few minutes to patch the tube. Inside her backpack, where she keeps her books, she slides out an air pump and fills the patched tire.

If I ever did get lost in the ocean, I'd want Bailey there with me.

She grabs one of the handlebars, pulls up her bike, and throws her leg over the seat. "Do you still ride your bike?" She uses her feet to roll over to me.

"No, not really."

"Why not?"

"Well, I guess I don't have anyone to ride with."

Bailey stops. "You could ride by yourself if you want, you know?"

"Is that what you do?"

"Sometimes. I'm not going to stop because no one else wants to ride bikes."

I'd wondered. "You still go to the park?"

"No, I usually just ride around town now." She rests a foot on one of the pedals. Around us, some Art Club kids are making their way out the gate.

"Well, I better get going before the after-school teachers wonder where I am." I turn and walk toward the cafeteria.

"We should have sunflower seeds for Saturday. I can bring some. The brand you like is David, right?" Bailey asks. "The kind in the red, yellow, and blue bag."

"Yeah." I'm glad she remembered.

She waves goodbye.

10

When I open the front door on Saturday morning, Bailey's holding a jumbo-size bag of sunflower seeds. "We have a lot of work to do. We're going to need it."

In the kitchen, she sets the bag in the middle of the table. I have the butcher paper and pencils set up. "Did you want something to drink? We have water, juice, root beer?"

"Root beer!" Mom yells from the living room.

Bailey sticks her head around the corner. "Hello, Mrs. Rodrigues." But Mom doesn't say anything.

It's been at least a year since Bailey's been to my house.

"Come on." She follows me into the living room, and we sit down on the couch. "Mom, Bailey's here."

Bailey reaches out her hand, and Mom takes it. "Hi," Bailey says.

I wonder how different Mom looks to her, how much she has changed.

"Cassie and I are working on an art project," Bailey adds, probably not knowing what else to say.

I tap Mom on the shoulder to get her to look at me. "I'll bring you some root beer, and if you need anything, we'll be in the kitchen, okay?"

But when I get up, Bailey's still sitting on the couch. "My hand. She won't let go of it."

Mom's eyes are focused on the television. I bend down in front of her. "Mom, Bailey has to help me with something. Can you let go of her hand?"

"I want some crackers and cheese," she says.

"Okay." I place my hand on Mom's and Bailey's. "Can you let go?" I ask her again.

But her grip tightens.

"Mom, please let go."

"When's Thanksgiving?" she asks out of nowhere. Her eyes shift to staring at the wall, at her portrait I drew.

"Not for another seven months." I try to gently pry Mom's and Bailey's hands apart.

"We have to get a turkey. Only up to a ten-pound turkey can fit in the oven. And don't forget to use half-and-half, not milk, in the mashed potatoes."

Mom must seem like a stranger to Bailey. "Are you doing okay?" I ask her.

She nods. "I didn't know she was—"

"And," Mom interrupts, "tell your dad not to wait until the night before to go to the store to get a turkey. There won't be any left, and we'll have to go to Kentucky Fried Chicken to get our dinner."

"Don't worry; I'll tell him."

Mom's grip is so strong. "I'm going to go get some crackers," I tell Bailey.

I go to the kitchen, make a plate of Ritz with Easy Cheese, and take it to the living room. As I set it on Mom's lap, I'm relieved she lets go of Bailey's hand and grabs a cracker.

Back at the kitchen table, Bailey rubs her hand. "Your mom's strong."

"I'm sorry," I say. I grab two root beers from the refrigerator.

"It's okay, really. I didn't know she was like that. I mean, I didn't know . . ." Bailey looks over her shoulder toward the living room.

"It would be that bad?"

"I'm sorry." Then she says something I didn't see coming. "My sister tells me stories of when Mom was alive and what she went through. I was too young to remember anything. When she tells the stories, she starts to cry. I feel bad because I don't have any of her memories. I missed out on knowing her, so I guess I don't feel sadness like my sister does. Or like you probably do?"

Bailey opens her can of root beer. "I don't know if that's good or bad. And I know it's not the same as with your mom."

"Doesn't have to be good or bad. It just is." I take a sip of my soda. It's more than she's actually ever told me. And that's something. "Okay, should we just start drawing what we want, or should we make a plan?"

"I think we should draw what we want and then go from there," Bailey says. "Mrs. G said she wanted our own perspective, so . . ."

There's a crash from the living room and a thump like something hitting the ground.

My portrait of Mom is on the floor, the frame broken, the glass cracked. She's staring at it like she's trying to figure out who the person in the sketch is. She gets down on her knees to take a closer look.

I grab it, and she reaches for the frame. "I want to see it."

"It's broken. You broke it, Mom." And then I ask a question I know she can't answer. "Why'd you do that?"

"I want to see it," she says again. "Is that me?"

"Yes, it's you." I take the picture and set it on the kitchen table. "But you can't see it. The glass is broken. You might cut yourself."

"Where's a broom?" Bailey asks.

"Thanks, but I'm an expert at sweeping up broken glass."

Mom's still standing where the picture fell. I sweep around her slippers.

Bailey holds the dustpan for me.

"She doesn't know my name," I say. She's the first person I've told. I bend down, lift what's left of the frame, and set it on the kitchen table next to the portrait.

"Does she still know who you are, though?" Bailey opens the cupboard under the sink. She remembers where the garbage is.

"Most of the time, I think."

The front door opens and closes. The clock reads 11:18, too early for Dad to be home.

"Come on," I say to Bailey, and we follow Mom outside.

Today there are patches of clouds in the sky, but the sun shines bright, and my favorite smells—sagebrush and piñon—fill the air. The summit of Mom's mountain is clear, the range more blue than purple.

We stop where the road meets the desert. I reach for the beach chairs hidden behind the sagebrush. I give one to Bailey, and we start to unfold them, but Mom keeps walking.

If Dad knew we were out here again, he'd never let

Mom go anywhere with just me again, not even a walk down the street.

But I have Bailey, and she and I walk on either side of her.

"Does she know the canyon's ahead of us?" Bailey asks.

"Yes, I do," Mom answers.

We go to the same spot where we were the other day, and Mom takes off her shoes, lies down again, and closes her eyes.

Bailey and I take off our shoes, too, but I sit up. Even though Bailey's here, I don't want to fall asleep.

"Do you know the story of the Lady of the Red Canyon?" Bailey asks. "My grandma told it to me."

"The lady disappeared, didn't she?"

"She jumped off the edge of the canyon," Mom says, "and people thought she died. But one day her son hiked down to the canyon, to the river. He stood on the bank and cried because his mom loved the river and the water; the currents made him think of only her."

It's weird, the things she does remember. Mom stops, and Bailey and I both wait for her to continue the story. "Mom, are you going to tell us the rest?"

"No, your friend can."

"Yeah, I can," Bailey agrees. She doesn't acknowledge that Mom's forgotten her name, too. "The son is at the edge of the river crying, and he hears a hawk. He looks up, and the hawk circles around him. The son shields his eyes from the sunlight, and he sees pieces of green falling from the sky. He catches them and sees that they're pieces of cloth. His mom's favorite color was green. This makes him cry more. He stuffs the cloths in all the pockets he has, and for the rest of the day, as he wanders up the river, his memory is filled with images of his mom.

"When night comes, he's too tired to go back home, so he falls asleep by the water's edge, and when he wakes up in the morning, he checks to make sure he still has the pieces of green cloth, but they're gone.

"He doesn't feel sad, though. As he makes his way back home, he hears her voice say to him, 'The sun is shining.'

"That's the end," Bailey says. "My grandma says she thinks about the story when she feels sad about my mom."

"Did they ever find out what happened to the lady?" I ask.

"No, she just disappeared."

The word "disappeared" scares me.

Bailey looks out at the canyon. "I've never done this before. Sat out here. It's nice."

"I like it," Mom says.

Bailey lies down next to her. "The sky is really blue today."

"It is." Mom opens her eyes, then closes them again. "And the sun is shining."

If I was out walking the canyon, and something of Mom's fell from the sky, it would probably be pieces of her favorite dress.

"You know . . . maybe the broken frame is a sign," Bailey says.

"A sign?"

"Yeah, like maybe you're supposed to replace the portrait with something new?"

I remember the day I drew the sketch. It was a month before the art show—April, the same time it is now—and I wanted to enter a portrait, so I asked Mom to be my subject. She, of course, said, "Absolutely!"

"Or it's a sign I should replace it with another one of her," I say to Bailey. "It would look different, though."

"How? She looks the same to me." Bailey's being nice.

"Does she? I'd have to look at pictures to know for sure. From here, to me, she doesn't look the same at all."

Mom's a collage now, kind of like the lady in the story Bailey told.

Maybe Bailey sees Mom as "the same Mrs. Rodrigues" because she's able to see her as the whole person she's always been. I wish I could do that, but it's all about perspective.

I don't know how long we stay out by the canyon, but I want to get back before Dad's home. Bailey and I slip our feet inside our shoes, and I help Mom with hers.

At home, I grab three bottles of water from the fridge and hand one to Bailey. "We haven't done much drawing," I tell her. "Maybe we can get together at your house? I mean, if we don't finish it at school."

"That'd be good." Bailey says, and we go out to the living room. I twist open the water bottle for Mom.

"It's like you're the mom, huh?" Bailey asks.

I forget how much Bailey notices things, how much she understands. "Yeah, it's been like that a lot more."

As we walk back to the kitchen, we stop in front of the broken frame.

"When I said you could replace it, I didn't mean forever," Bailey says.

"No, I knew what you meant, like maybe it's time for something new." But I'm not sure I'm ready for that.

"You can still have this one. All you have to do is get a new frame."

She's right. The actual sketch isn't damaged at all. "Yeah, I can fix it."

But I don't want Dad to see it before I tell him what happened. I take the broken frame to my room and slide it under my bed.

"I thought it was your mom who liked ocean stuff?"

Bailey stares at the ocean poster and at the ceiling over my bed where a dolphin poster hangs. It's a photograph of a real one, with just its head poking out of the water.

"In every picture I've seen of dolphins," Bailey says as she sits down in front of my desk, "why do they always look like they're smiling?"

"My mom would say it's because being a dolphin would make you happy pretty much all the time."

"Is your mom the reason you wanted to paint the ocean mural?"

"Yeah, I guess so." And then I say, "It's weird to be around someone losing her memory."

"I'm sorry," Bailey says. I guess it's her turn now.

I stare up at the word "dream" on the bottom of the poster. "I'm always wondering now—what her dreams are like. You know how a regular person's dreams are filled with images of what happened to them that day or what happened to them last week or last year?"

I sit down on my bed. "Since those images are unreachable for my mom, I think her dreams are filled with the ocean. The whole time she's asleep, all she sees is ocean life or a dolphin breaching the water, swimming for miles and miles. It's kind of like those videos of a fireplace people have on their TVs or tanks with colorful fish swimming, trying to create a feeling of calm."

Bailey and I both stare up at the poster, like I do most

nights. It makes it easy to fall asleep, knowing that maybe that's what Mom sees, too, when she closes her eyes.

Someday I'm going to take it down, though.

"I want to take my mom to swim with dolphins for real." I grab the bowl of broken pieces from my desk and set it on the floor. "My dad doesn't think it's a good idea, but I'm still trying to convince him."

"Where do you have to go?" Bailey asks.

"San Diego."

She picks up one of the pieces—a red fluke. "That's not too far."

"No, it isn't. Mom and I could take the bus."

Bailey sits on the floor and searches through pieces, looking for two that fit together. "What if your dad keeps saying no?"

"I could take her myself."

"You'd do that?" She's surprised, but not in a bad way.

It'd be like jumping in the deep end, except I would have a plan, an idea of what's coming. "Yep, I would."

A BAD DAY

When Mom comes into the cafeteria, I'm sitting at a table, my head covered by my sweatshirt hood, most of my face burrowed inside my arms. I must look like a rock. I don't get up at first, so she walks over to me, bends down, and starts singing "Girls Just Want to Have Fun" quietly. I want to stay mad, but the song always makes me feel a little better.

She keeps singing on our way to the car. I'm sure she noticed my eyes, that I've been crying. If I had sunglasses, I'd be wearing them now. She usually encourages me to sing along, but not today. At the end of the song, as the words fade, she asks, "How was your day?"

"It wasn't good." If I'd said, "It was fine," she would have known I wasn't telling the truth.

"I'm sorry. Do you want to talk about it?"

"Not really. It's just one of those days."

"Do you think we should go get ice cream?"

"Not in the mood."

"Well." Mom leans over the steering wheel, her driving position of choice. "Maybe you might want to talk about it later."

"I don't know. It was one little thing, anyway . . . but it kinda ruined the rest of the day." I slide the hood off my head.

When we get home, I've barely set my backpack down before Mom says, "Come on. We're going back out."

She has something tucked inside her jacket.

"Where we going?" I ask.

"You know."

"To the canyon."

Mom gives me a thumbs-up.

"What are you hiding in your jacket?" I catch up to her. She's a fast walker.

"It's a surprise."

The sky is clear, the blue deep, not ocean-deep but the kind that reminds me of my mom's and dad's hugs.

At the end of the road, we step onto the desert floor. I see the silhouette of a hawk, circling against the blue, the dark green of the sagebrush, and the brown and red of the dirt. I wonder how many footprints Mom, Dad, and I have left here.

About ten yards from the edge of the canyon, Mom sits down. She pulls something from the inside of her jacket. I know what it is immediately.

"The book you always used to read to me," I say.

"*You Are My Sunshine*," Mom says. "A great book of philosophy."

It's about a group of animals who live in a forest. One is sad, and his friends do everything they can to cheer him up, but nothing works. They keep showing they're there for him, though, and eventually the sun comes out.

"You must've read it to me a lot of times, because I can remember the whole thing."

"I did. Sometimes I needed to hear the story, too."

I lie down and listen to her read it again. When she finishes, she lies next to me. "You feel any better?" she asks.

"I feel okay."

Mom finds my hand and squeezes it. "How do you think Georgia O'Keeffe would paint this sky?"

"I mean, I could guess, but I definitely know how *I'd* paint it." I sit up. The sky out here looks like it goes on forever. It's the kind of sky people see in their dreams. If I were Georgia O'Keeffe, I'd focus on color. The shades of blue are what make it magical. Blues of sadness, of vastness, of cool, of peace, all mixed together.

"I'd get the color right first, and then at the bottom of

the canvas, I'd paint a mountain—just the very top of it—and in the middle would be two arms, tangled together like they're trying to hug the sky."

"What would the title be?" Mom asks.

"Hmm . . . *Desert Sky*?"

"How 'bout *Cassie's Sky*?"

"That would be perfect." I lie back down, and it's quiet except for a breeze, whistling, a sound that belongs to only the wind.

"How would you paint the sky?" I ask her.

"I'm not an artist."

"You can use your imagination."

Mom doesn't answer right away. Maybe she's waiting for the wind to carry an answer to her. "I got it! It would be blue, of course, but there would be all sorts of small objects floating against the blue, like our house, a swim cap, goggles, Dad's favorite sweater, my favorite swimsuit, your hiking boots and paintbrushes and the yellow dress with pink flowers you wore every day when you were four years old. And there'd have to be at least one dolphin."

"What would the title be?"

"*Swimming in Things that Give Me Life*. Good?"

"It's good." I scoot closer to Mom, our shoulders touching. "Thanks for bringing me out here."

"Anytime," she says. "Anytime."

"We can go whenever you're ready," I tell her.

"I'm not ready just yet."

Me neither. Out here, it's not just the sky that seems to go on forever, Time does, too. I think it's because we're next to the canyon, with its layers of rock that are millions of years old. I'm convinced the canyon stops Time. An hour, a day, a week, or a month seems like nothing compared to a million years. Each is a speck of sand compared to a mountain. They're a drop of water compared to an ocean.

But at the same time, this day, right now, with Mom beside me, with the sound of her voice reading *You Are My Sunshine* or humming "Girls Just Want to Have Fun," is everything, everything under the cool, peaceful vastness of blue.

Mom stands up, brushing the dirt off her pants. "You want to help me make dinner tonight?" She offers her hand to me and helps pull me to my feet.

"Sure."

"But we have to do one thing before we leave." She holds her hand up. I do the same, and we "touch" the mountains.

When we get back to the road, streetlights turn on, shining with an orangish glow, and headlights from cars, too. People are coming home from work, dogs are barking, and front doors are opening and closing. Our porch light is glowing yellow, the same shade as the swim cap I've seen Mom wear.

As we get to the sidewalk, leading to the front door, she grabs my hand. "Bad day made better, right?"

"Definitely."

I'm not sure what I'd do without her.

11

Dad's already made Mom breakfast. They're sitting at the table, and he's resting his face against one hand, turning an empty coffee mug around and around with the other.

"You want some more coffee?" I ask him.

"No . . . thanks."

"What's wrong?" I drop my backpack next to my chair.

"Have some breakfast," he says, looking up at the clock, "and then I'll take you to school."

I grab butter and jelly from the refrigerator.

"That's good," Dad says.

"I didn't say anything." Today it's my turn to give him a concerned look. "Dad, I know something's wrong."

"We'll talk about it later." He sets his coffee mug in the sink and kisses me on the forehead.

But I won't let it go. "I want to know now, because I'll think about what it is all day, and whatever I think is probably going to be ten times worse than what it actually is. So tell me, please."

He sighs. "Okay." I know it's going to be something heavy, because he has to take a deep breath.

"I think it's time, Cassie," he says.

It's time.

"I've been thinking about this a lot. It's not Mrs. Collins's fault she can't keep Mom from doing the things she does. And my main concern is keeping your mom safe . . . even safe from herself. So . . ."

I know what he's going to say. "We have to put her in a home." Dad explained this to me when Mom got sick, that someday we might have to put her in a "care facility." That seems like a long time ago but also not that long at all.

"It might take a while for a space to open up. I want to get her into High Desert Village. It's right across town, so she'll be close. They have a waiting list."

"So it definitely won't be right away?" I ask. "Summer's coming, and—"

"I don't know exactly when." I don't like this answer, but the look on his face tells me it's the truth.

I try something else. "Before she goes, can we take her

to San Diego? I read Mom's bucket list again, and the only thing in her top five that's realistic is swimming with dolphins."

"Yeah, I guess we can't take her to England or Peru," he says, staring at the floor like he's remembering a time when we could go wherever we wanted.

"Well, we can . . ." We could still do a lot. We could go get ice cream, visit an art museum, or just get in the car and drive.

"And the dolphins . . . ?" I nudge. I can predict his response, but I need to ask one more time.

"Cassie, I just don't think—"

"I know. You've made your decision."

So Dad's not going to help. But it doesn't matter. I'm going to figure out a way.

Later, on the way to school, the DJ on the radio is making jokes. Dad turns it off, and I'm glad; I don't want to hear people laughing, either. "You going to be okay?" he asks.

I give him an honest answer. "I'm not right now."

"I should've waited to tell you."

"I wanted to know," I say, and it's true. Now I know I'm running out of time.

Dad stops the car, and I grab my back pack as I open the back door, waving as he drives off.

On the first day of school, Mrs. G told us she had two goals for everyone in our class. One: *I want you to get over any fear you may have about asking questions.* Two: *No matter what subject we're studying, I want you to understand what exactly is being asked of you. I want you to be able to break down a question and understand its parts, whether that question is in math, reading, writing, social studies, or science. How can we solve a problem if we don't know what's involved?* she'd said.

Plans are like that, too. Making plans requires the ability to break down an idea into a step-by-step recipe of actions needed to get from one point to the other. So, during math, I outline a plan to get Mom to San Diego.

There's a bus that leaves at eight thirty. We'd need to be at the station by eight o'clock. That means we'd have to leave the house right after Dad left for work, which is seven thirty.

I'd have a backpack ready, and I'd pedal Mom to the bus station. My bike's a one-seater, so I'd let Mom sit on the seat while I stood and pedaled. Once we were at the bus station, I'd leave my bike . . .

But this is where my plans stop. I don't know if the

station has a bike rack, and even if I did leave my bike there, there's a chance it'd be gone when I got back. Then I'd have to call Dad to come pick us up. I don't want to have to do that.

"Cassie, can you give us the quotient, please?" Mrs. G's voice is far away.

"What number are we on?" I'm still trying to figure out what I'm going to do with my bike.

"3c."

I'd started planning after 3b. I read question c. I'm good at math; I can usually do it quickly. I try to focus on the question, but I can't. *When Mom goes to High Desert Village, what's it going to be like living in our house without her?* I don't want to cry, not now.

Plans, bikes, math. *Focus.*

"I don't know, Mrs. G. Sorry. I don't have an answer."

"It's okay, Cassie." She calls on someone else.

During recess, Bailey asks me if I want to play soccer, but I don't feel like running, or kicking, or doing anything but sitting on the sidelines.

"You should play!" Bailey yells.

"Maybe later."

Bailey shrugs.

After school during Art Club, everyone is working on their practice panels for the mural, hovering over their butcher paper, hiding their drawings from the rest of us. I can't see what Bailey's drawing, either. My guess is flowers, maybe a jackrabbit or a roadrunner, and then in the background, desert and sky.

My part of the mural will have a saguaro cactus with five arms. In the middle of the cactus's trunk, I draw a hole. I've seen them when we're out hiking; they're usually made by woodpeckers, and when the woodpeckers leave, owls or other birds like sparrows or finches move in and use them as nests. But I'm not drawing any birds—well, maybe one, an elf owl perched either at the top of the cactus or on a spine, its head tilted to the side so that it looks like it's peering inside the hole.

By the time I finish the arms, the saguaro takes up most of the space, with just a little room left for the sky.

When Art Club is over, I pick up my graphite pencils.

"I love saguaros," Bailey says. On her side of the panel, she's drawn four of them, each with a single flower growing on one of its arms. "I'm going to paint the flowers different colors."

"Nice. They'll look beautiful."

"If you think we're ready, we can start our final sketch at my house?"

I haven't been to Bailey's house in a while. It feels normal, and a little normal is nice to get back to. "Yeah, we can do that." I slip my arms through my backpack. Bailey grabs a fresh piece of butcher paper, and we walk out of the classroom together. "I'll finish my practice one at home and bring it. I want to fill the hole in the cactus. Just haven't decided whether it's going to be animals or something else."

After school, when I get to the cafeteria, everyone's playing outside. I find a spot at a table, take out my pencils, and finish my drawing. At the bottom of the cactus's nest, I draw a stingray and then an octopus, two of its arms attached to the edge of the nest. Between them, in the background, is a dolphin, swimming toward the inside of the cactus.

All those times at the beach, when Mom swam out just past where the surf was breaking, I should've swum with her. It wasn't far. Between the bottom of the ocean and the surface was probably no more than ten, fifteen feet, and even though I wouldn't have been able to touch the bottom, she would have been there.

Instead, I twisted my feet deep into the wet sand and clenched my toes, like roots of a tree, holding me in place. Standing there, I thought my pink Santa Cruz hoodie would be a beacon for Mom, that if she ever got disoriented, she'd be able to look up and there would be me.

I erase the tip of the dolphin's dorsal fin and redraw it

so that it's more of a curve. Surrounding the stingray, octopus, and dolphin will be ocean, and behind the cactus will be sky, two shades of blue.

Someone—Jonathan—will say something. "Those animals don't live in the desert." Yes, I know. "It's supposed to be a desert mural." For the most part, it is. "We voted on a desert theme." Yes, but Mrs. G said our part of the mural should be from our own point of view.

This is mine.

It's Saturday morning. I told Bailey I'd be at her house by ten. I hear Mom's feet in the hallway, shuffling across the floor. That's one thing that's stayed the same; she's always dragged her feet. She does it when she's at the beach, too, kicking sand with each step.

I glue two more dolphins together, then go to my closet and twist open the lid of the Mason jar I use as a bank. I slide out all the cash money I've saved and stuff it inside my backpack.

You need a credit card to make reservations at the aquatic center, and of course I can't use Dad's. But I have an idea.

Dad and Mom are in the living room, sitting next to each other on the couch. I kiss Mom on the cheek and kiss him on the cheek, too. "I'll be back in a few hours."

"Have fun," he says.

My bike's in the garage. I push it out to the driveway and ride down the road.

Bailey's yard is covered with different types of cacti. Yellow and pink flowers bloom, hiding their thorns. I grin at the sight of the bright colors and the smell of Grandma Lorena's rice and beans. I'd know that smell anywhere. She loves to cook when people come over.

Bailey opens the door before I have a chance to knock. We go to the kitchen. Lorena is already scooping beans into bowls. "Cassandra!" she says. "It's been a long time. Sit down. Hope you didn't have breakfast yet."

I did, but I always have room for whatever Grandma Lorena is cooking.

"How is your mom?" she asks.

"Grandma . . . ," Bailey says. I guess she told her about Mom.

"It's good to talk about sad things. I've taught you that, Miss Bailey, haven't I?" Grandma Lorena sets tortillas and another bowl—this one filled with fresh salsa—on the table.

"It's okay. She's not doing that great." I take a spoonful of salsa and drop it on top of my beans. "I guess she has her good and bad days."

I'm thinking about Dad putting Mom in a home, and

I start eating the beans and rice to keep myself from crying.

"I'm sorry," Grandma Lorena says. She looks to the sky and makes the sign of the cross.

She pours us glasses of pineapple juice. I'm thirstier than I thought, and I gulp it down. It's more sour than sweet. It's good.

As we eat our beans, Grandma Lorena hovers over us, asking if we need anything else. I don't mind. I love sitting in this kitchen. The walls are painted the same shade of yellow as the cactus flowers outside, and there are colorful ceramic pots hanging from the ceiling. The bud-like leaves are like drops of rain.

Grandma Lorena is older than my mom, but she remembers my name, even after not seeing me in a while. She's cooked this meal. Her eyes are here, not far away, and I know whatever she says next will be normal, expected, nothing I have to prepare myself for.

When I'm finished with my beans, she asks if I want more. "Maybe before I leave," I tell her.

"That's a good answer." Bailey smiles.

Grandma Lorena agrees and promises to send me home with extra for Mom and Dad, too.

We take our bowls to the sink and go to the living room. The walls are magenta, reminding me of a desert sunset, and more pots with colorful designs hang from the ceiling, their plants with leaves that remind me of lizards' feet.

"Ready to get to work?" Bailey's made a space for us at the coffee table. The butcher paper we'll use for our final drawing is rolled out flat, and pencils and paints sit at its edge.

Oh. "I messed up," I say. "I forgot to bring our practice one." I was thinking about Mom. "I know where I left it—I'll run home. I'm sorry."

But Bailey doesn't seem worried, and that makes me feel okay, too. "Do we need it?" she asks. "I remember what I drew."

"I do, too."

Grandma Lorena brings us a bowl of pistachios and more pineapple juice, then waves to us as she walks back to the kitchen.

"I missed coming here," I say.

"Maybe you missed my grandma's cooking more?" Bailey smiles.

I laugh. "I definitely missed that."

A door opens from the hallway, and Sonia, Bailey's older sister, walks out. She has long black hair like Bailey's, her skin the same shade of brown.

"Good morning, Cassie," Sonia says and plops down

on the couch next to me. She gently tugs Bailey's hair. "Good to see you."

"It's almost afternoon." Bailey leans back against Sonia's legs.

"You know I worked late last night. And I'm hungry." Sonia gets up and heads toward the kitchen. "Beans, yes!" She raises her fist in victory.

Bailey motions to the paper. "We should work on our panel," she says.

But first . . . "Do you remember when I told you about wanting to take my mom to swim with dolphins in San Diego?"

"Yeah." Her face lights up.

I riffle inside my backpack and take out the money I stashed in one of the pockets, setting it on the table. "There's enough here to pay for one person—I can just watch—and a night at a hotel for both of us. I just need a credit card to hold the reservation. Do you think your grandma would mind helping me?"

"She might tell your dad. She'd be worried about you," says Bailey. "But . . ." She pauses. "What about Sonia?"

I'm not sure how that'd be any different, but before I can say so or think about it too much, Sonia plops onto the couch with a bowl of beans. "I heard my name."

"Cassie needs your help," Bailey says. "Tell her."

So I do.

"I'm sorry about your mom," Sonia says when I'm finished. I'm sure there's a "but" coming and she's not going to help me.

Instead, she continues. "When our mom was alive . . . well, when she first got sick, when Bailey was just two years old, she'd tell me she wanted to take us to Disney World. She said if she could close her eyes and have the power to transport us anywhere, that's where she'd go." Sonia hands Bailey her bowl. "I wouldn't have thought twice about taking her there myself if I could have."

She goes to her room and comes back out carrying her laptop. "Let's make some reservations."

I let out a breath I didn't realize I was holding. "Thank you."

This was exactly what I wanted, but watching her make the reservations, I'm nervous. This is really going to happen, and it's going to happen without my dad. I get a funny feeling in my stomach, and I can hear his voice. "What if something happens? What if your mom runs off? What if you're at the aquatic center and she gets upset?"

But what if it's an amazing trip? And if I don't do it now, it'll never happen.

Before I leave, I ask Bailey if she'll go over the plans with me. I explain about getting us to the bus station on my bike.

"Well," Bailey says right away, "if it helps, you can use my bike. I put a new seat on it, a longer one, so there's more space for two people." She reaches for the pistachios. "I can bring it to you, but if your dad sees it, he'll probably wonder why it's there."

"I could hide it." I'd have to think about where.

"Or I can bring it to you right before you plan to leave?" Bailey asks. "Plus, there isn't a bike rack at the station. Sonia and I have to pick up my uncle there when he comes to visit us. I know a shortcut, too. Once we're there, I'll take both bikes home, and when you come back on the bus, I'll be waiting for you with them."

She stops talking. "That is, if you want me to come with you. I didn't mean to take over your plans."

"It's fine," I say. "They're good ideas. I should have asked for your help from the beginning."

There's not much to the rest of my plan, but I go through it anyway. "The bus is supposed to leave at nine o'clock. My dad leaves for work at seven thirty."

We decide Bailey will get the two bikes—she said she'd have no trouble riding one and holding the other one next to her—to my house by twenty minutes before eight o'clock. Mom and I will be dressed, and I'll have our bus tickets, snacks for the trip, and a bag with some clothes already packed. Bailey will knock five times so I know she's here. She'll carry the backpack with her, and we'll ride away. If everything goes smoothly.

I realize I can't remember the last time Mom was on a bike. It might freak her out, or she might think it's the best thing in the world. I have to be ready for anything.

Once we're at the station, we'll say our goodbyes. Mom and I will board our bus. Once we get to San Diego, I'll use my leftover money for a taxi ride to Aquatic Park. If we don't hit traffic, it'll take us about four hours to get to San Diego. Then it's another thirty minutes to the park. Our appointment is at two o'clock.

After Mom gets to swim, we'll go to a motel. I'll have to call Dad. I'll need to explain to him where we are and what I did. He'll be mad. He'll think I put Mom and myself in a dangerous, unpredictable situation. "But," I'll say, "life is unpredictable, Dad, right?"

"Think you have everything covered," Bailey says. She throws a pistachio in the air and catches it in her mouth. "But we barely worked on the mural."

"We still have time."

But Mom doesn't. So I'm glad I'm helping her make at least one dream come true.

12

During dinner on Sunday, Dad tells me he's asked Mrs. Collins to come over and stay with Mom and me over spring break.

That does not work with my plan. "Why?"

"I just think it'd be a good idea to have her here. That way if you and Bailey want to get together, you can, and you won't have to stay with Mom."

The next morning, I still haven't figured out what I'm going to do about Mrs. Collins, but I keep to the rest of my plan. I get up at the same time as when I go to school, but I don't walk out of my room. I let Dad think I'm sleeping in. I hear the clanking of coffee cups, then water running through pipes. He's taking a shower. I peer out to see where Mom is. Dad's made her breakfast this morning, her crackers and cheese, and she's sitting in the living room watching TV. The running water stops, and I go back to my room.

My backpack, stuffed with clothes, snacks, water, and Mom's medications, is in the corner of my closet, ready to go. I'm already dressed, but I hop under the covers because I want to make Dad think I'm still asleep. He knocks on my door. "Cassie, I'm going." I don't answer at first. "Cassie? Mom's watching TV. If you need anything, Mrs. Collins will be here around nine, okay?"

"Okay."

"And you can always call me."

I poke my head out from under the covers and say, "Yeah, I will."

I don't get up until I hear the front door close. Soon as I get to the living room, I look out the front window to make sure Dad's left. It's seven thirty. Mom's still in her pajamas; since I'm home, he left it to me to get her dressed. I make a quick breakfast, butter, peanut butter, and cinnamon on toast, but I can't eat any of it, not even one piece. I'm nervous, my stomach in knots.

I get dressed and then pick out some clothes for Mom. When I get to the living room, I take her hand and bend down next to her. "Mom, it's time to get dressed." She keeps her eyes on the TV. "Mom." I hold her clothes in the air. "We have to get dressed. I'm taking you somewhere."

"Where?" she asks, now looking at the clothes.

"We're going to see some dolphins." I wait for her to give me a kiss on the forehead or a hug, but there's no reaction. I know she'll be happy when we get there.

For the most part, Mom can dress herself, but I stay next to her in case she needs me, and I tie her shoelaces. I grab our jackets and double-check to make sure I have everything I think we'll need in my backpack, including Mom's bathing suit. On the kitchen table, I leave a note: *"Good morning, Mrs. Collins. Mom and I went over to my friend Bailey's house. We'll be back in a couple of hours. Please don't worry. I'll call later."* I draw a smiley face and sign my name.

Bailey knocks on the door, and I open it.

"Ready?" she asked.

I turn off the lights and TV and make sure everything is just as Dad wants it to be when we leave the house.

"Mom," I say to her, "remember Bailey?"

"Hi, Mrs. Rodrigues." Bailey holds out her hand to shake, but Mom just nods and says she likes Bailey's sweatshirt, a black one with a picture of a wave. "Thanks," Bailey says.

The bikes are leaning against the side of the house. Bailey takes my backpack to carry and helps Mom get on the back of the banana seat. She's too tall, and her feet are going to drag on the ground. "Mrs. Rodrigues," Bailey says, "you're going to want to lift your feet a little. Okay? It won't be for long. The bus station isn't that far."

Mom nods. "I haven't been on a bike for a long time."

My first thought as we pedal down our dirt driveway is that I hope no one we know sees us. I should've brought a couple of baseball caps for Mom and me to wear, but it's too late. I don't want to turn back now. I don't want to get even a little behind schedule.

I can feel Mom holding on to my hips. I look over my shoulder, and she's leaning her head out to the side so that she can feel the wind against her face. She has her eyes closed, and she is smiling.

Both Bailey and I are quiet until I say, "I had to lie, and I need you to cover for me. Dad told Mrs. Collins to come over to stay with my mom. I left her a note that says we're over your house. So . . ."

"So if she does call to check on you," Bailey says, "I have to tell her you're there."

"I'm sorry."

"If she asks to talk to you, I'll tell her we're making cookies or something and you have cookie dough all over your hands and that I'll have you call her back. Does that sound good?"

I'm not sure I deserve Bailey being such a good friend. "Thank you for doing that for me."

"You can owe me a bag of Takis."

"Think I should owe you more than one bag."

Bailey and I ride down streets through a part of town I've never been to. Most of the houses are a block apart from each other, and then there are parts of town, the newer parts, where they've built a couple of small subdivisions. The yards are nice, and everything has an order to it. Control. That's what the people who live there want to create, I think. As opposed to life. As opposed to watching someone you love lose her memory enough that she can't remember your name. Or lying to your dad so you can help your mom check something off her bucket list.

When my mom got sick, we lost the money she brought in from her job. And we had to spend extra money to hire Mrs. Collins. So we had to cut out some things that we'd gotten used to having. To be honest, it wasn't that hard. I haven't missed anything that I had before, except for my mom being my mom. Nothing else really matters.

"This is the last street we take until we get to the one the bus station's on," Bailey says.

She has a speedometer on her bike and keeps looking at it. "We have one point eight miles to go," she says. She's calculated the distance.

For the most part, Mom has kept her feet up, but every once in a while, she lets them fall, and the bottoms of her shoes scrape the road. There's a cadence in the sound she makes; I swear she's trying to play songs with the pattern she makes with her feet. "Girls Just Want to Have Fun," "Footloose," "Billie Jean." Now she's humming. She used to hum all the time, while she cooked breakfast or dinner, while she folded clothes, while she dusted.

She can remember the tunes to so many songs but has a hard time remembering my name. I take a breath. It's not that I'm mad at Mom, but I resent her illness. "There's a difference," I told Dad, "right?" I need to keep this thought in my head when I start to feel angry. All my mad needs to go toward the illness, not toward Mom.

"The bus station is in a couple of blocks," Bailey says.

There are buildings now instead of houses. Mom has stopped humming; she's quiet. I try to look back at her. The handlebars swerve a little, and her feet scrape the street. "Are you okay?" I ask.

"I'm fine. Are you okay?"

"I'm good." It's been a while since she's asked me how I am.

Bailey and I park our bikes along the side of the bus station. I help Mom get off, and Bailey gives me my backpack.

"You have everything you need?" she asks.

"Think so."

"Well, then, I guess I'll see you when you get back. Good luck." Bailey throws her leg up and around the seat of her own bike and holds the other bike with her right hand.

"Thanks, Bailey. Thanks for . . . being there."

I want to say more, but I think she knows. "Anytime. See ya!" She pedals away.

Watching her leave, I suddenly feel alone and a little scared. It's just Mom and me now. I lift my backpack onto my back, and we walk toward the bus.

13

Mom sits in a chair while I walk to the counter to check if our bus is on time.

"You're not traveling alone, are you?" the clerk asks.

"No, that's my mom over there." I point to where Mom's sitting.

"Is she okay?" Right now, Mom's just staring out the front window of the station.

"She likes to daydream," I say. "You said the bus will board in ten minutes?" I try to get his attention away from my mom.

"Yeah, we'll make an announcement, and you'll board right through those doors."

"Thank you." I walk back over to where she's sitting. "You hungry? I have some crackers." I hold up two Ziploc bags of Ritz and Saltines. Mom takes the Ritz. She opens the bag herself and eats two at a time.

I hope I brought enough snacks. I can remember the stories Mom used to tell about me as a two-year-old. "You always wanted a cup full of oyster crackers. You know the kind; they're round, taste salty. Restaurants serve them when you order clam chowder. Anyway, you'd walk around the house with a cupful, and when you ran out, you'd walk into the kitchen and point to the cupboard where I kept the crackers, and you'd say, 'More, please.'"

The clerk comes over the loudspeaker and announces that our bus is boarding.

On the bus, I let Mom sit next to the window. I set her up with more crackers and a bottle of water. From my backpack, I take out an iPod and headphones. Music should keep Mom occupied. She puts headphones over her ears and pushes Play.

"Ladies and gentlemen." The bus driver comes on the loudspeaker. I open my eyes. "We've just entered San Diego."

I look over at the seat where Mom's supposed to be sitting, but she's not there. I start to worry but realize there's not a whole lot of places she could've gone. We're on a bus.

I peer down the aisle and don't see her. She's probably in the bathroom.

The door says LOCKED. I knock softly, not wanting to

draw attention to myself from the other passengers. "Mom?" I whisper.

There's no answer. "Mom?" I say again and listen for any sound coming from inside.

I knock again. "Mom?" I lean my shoulder into the door and realize she can't hear me because she's still listening to music.

I wait for her outside the door. When she opens it, she says, "Hello," like I'm a stranger.

———————

Once we get off the bus, I spot taxicabs waiting in front of the station. Mom's still wearing her headphones. If music makes her happy, she can wear them as long as she needs to.

We get in a taxi, and I tell the driver to take us to the aquatic park. It should take about thirty minutes.

When we arrive, there aren't many cars in the parking lot. The main building looks closed, but I checked online to make sure they'd be open, and they accepted my reservation, so it must not be.

As we're almost to the front doors—now I see lights on inside—my cell phone rings. The only person who would call me is Dad.

"Hi," I say in my try-to-talk-as-normally-as-possible voice.

"Where are you? Are you okay? Mrs. Collins called and said you've been over at Bailey's for a long time."

"We're fine. Yeah, we're still over Bailey's," I lie. "We're making cookies, and we got carried away."

"How's your mom? Let me talk to her."

I lift one of the headphones and press my phone to Mom's ear.

I can hear Dad say, "Hi, Kim. Are you baking cookies?"

He knows there's a fifty-fifty chance Mom won't respond. He pauses and waits for a minute. She doesn't say anything.

"Kim, are you at Bailey's house?"

Mom yells, "There's a dolphin!" She points to the big front window. Hanging from the ceiling in the lobby area is a life-size model of a bottlenose dolphin.

"Kim!" I can hear Dad say through the phone. "Kim!"

But Mom is busy staring through the glass. I take back the phone. "Hi, Dad, don't worry. Mom's just watching a dolphin show we put on for her. She got bored making cookies."

"Is it a new one?" he asks. "She doesn't usually react that way unless it's something she hasn't seen before."

"Yeah." I come up with a good lie. "Actually, just so happens that Bailey's sister, Sonia, loves dolphins, too, so she has some DVDs that Mom hasn't seen."

That seems to be enough. "Okay," Dad says. "I'm going to call later to check on things."

"That's fine."

"Stay ten more minutes," he says, "and then go home. Promise me."

"I promise. Bye." I hang up. *I will be calling you in*—I look at the time on my phone—*about two hours.*

Inside the lobby, Mom stands right under the dolphin model, looking up. She has this amazing smile on her face. She lifts both her arms in the air and reaches up on her tiptoes, trying to touch the model.

There are a few people in the lobby with us, and they stare at Mom. I know what they're thinking. At first, when Mom behaved like a kid in public—when Dad still let us bring her places—I would be embarrassed, but now, because I've gotten used to the stares, I tend to join her— as long as it's not too embarrassing. If she's loud, I'll try to get her to go outside. I like seeing her excited about things. It reminds me of who she used to be.

I stand next to her, lift up on my tiptoes, and reach my fingertips to the dolphin, too.

Mom starts listing facts about dolphins. She sounds like she should be working at a place like this.

I sit down on the edge of a small fountain that's in the middle of the lobby. When it gets close to our reservation time, I walk up to the window and then ask where we need to go.

"Mom." I tap her on the shoulder. "Mom!" She doesn't respond because she's still mesmerized by the dolphin model.

"We're going to go swimming," I tell her. But she won't take her eyes off the dolphin.

"Mom." I stand in front of her and move my arms like I'm swimming the butterfly stroke. "Let's go swim."

"Your arms need to be a little more bent at the elbows when you're swimming the butterfly," she says. So that she remembers, too.

"Maybe you can show me when you get in the water," I say.

The dolphin pools are at the back of the park. We walk into a stadium-like building and go through a short tunnel. I can hear splashing. Mom stops. Then we hear the clicks.

She gets another amazing smile on her face. "Dolphins," she whispers.

This makes me happy, too.

We make it through the tunnel. In the middle of the stadium is a huge pool where there are two dolphins swimming. There are a couple of what I think are trainers. They wear wet suits and stand next to buckets of fish.

Mom walks toward them, lifting her leg over the railing that separates the pool from the auditorium seats. She walks right up to the edge of the water and bends down.

I rush toward her, grabbing her arm.

One of the trainers runs over, too. She grabs Mom's other arm, but neither of us pulls. We both kneel beside her and let her look down into the water.

"Thank you," I say to the trainer. She has a kind smile.

"We have a reservation to swim with dolphins at two o'clock."

"Oh, are you Kim?"

"No." I point to Mom. "This is Kim."

Mom scoops the water with her hand. One of the dolphins swims up, breaches the surface, and throws its head back in a quick motion.

"That's Hannah," the trainer says. "She's saying 'hello.'"

It startles Mom at first. She squeezes her hand to her chest and watches Hannah breach the water again, but this time the dolphin comes out of the water, waist-high, and flips herself backward.

Mom is hypnotized by Hannah, wonder in her eyes.

The trainer extends her hand. "By the way, my name is Beth."

"Nice to meet you," I say and shake her hand. Beth tries to shake hands with Mom, but Mom's still mesmerized by Hannah.

I need to prepare Beth. "There's something you should know about my mom. She has Alzheimer's, and sometimes it doesn't seem like she's listening or understanding. But swimming with dolphins has always been her dream, so that's why we're here."

"Okay," Beth says. "Is there anything we should avoid?"

"No," I say, "I don't think so. I think once she gets in the water, she'll be so amazed that dolphins are right next to her, she'll be fine."

"Sounds good," Beth says. "Follow me so your mom can put on her suit. The water is a little chilly. But before you change, I'm going to give a short talk, going over general rules and some information about dolphins."

There are four other people who've signed up for the "Dolphin Interaction." Beth tells us about dolphins' anatomy and behavior and what they eat. When she finishes, she motions to a rack of wet suits.

"Your mom and I are probably the same size," she says to me. "I wear a medium. And you're not going in the water, right?" I nod.

I try to take Mom to the changing room, but it's clear she doesn't want to leave. "Mom," I say, "we're coming back. And you're going to get in the water with them!" That seems to calm her, and she follows.

Mom puts on her bathing suit easily, but when I show her the wet suit, she asks, "Why do I need that?"

"To keep you warm. The trainer said the water is cold."

"I don't want to wear that. I used to swim in the Pacific Ocean all the time without a wet suit when I was younger. I'm not wearing it, okay?"

I guess it will be okay.

She steps out of the changing room and darts toward the pool. Without waiting for Beth, she slips right in, without any hesitation. She dives down into the water.

"Kim?" Beth yells, but Mom can't hear her. She's at the bottom now. I can see her swimsuit with flowers on it, a red blur. She moves like a dolphin to the other side of the pool.

"That's not allowed . . . ," Beth says. I can tell she's not quite sure what to do. She's probably used to telling the parent that their kid isn't following the rules. "When she comes up, can you tell her that we're going to be in the other part of the pool?" Beth asks. "It's shallower. She can stand up and get really close to the animals."

I wait for Mom to come up for air. I see her nose and mouth break the surface, but then she goes right back under. She dives deep and swims using a dolphin kick motion again, her arms out in front of her. Hannah seems to reconsider her plan, and soon she's down there with Mom, swimming right next to her, and for as long as she can hold her breath, Mom is literally swimming with dolphins, moving the exact same way. If it were up to her, and this was the ocean rather than a swimming pool, I really believe she would keep swimming, that she would stop a little way from shore, stick her head above the surface, wave, throw me a kiss, and disappear under the surface again, away from what she knew.

Beth blows a whistle. It's to signal to Hannah that she's supposed to swim into the shallow part of the pool.

Mom comes up for air and looks down into the water, searching for Hannah, a bit of worry in her eyes.

"Mom!" I yell. She finally looks up at me, and I point to the shallow end. She swims over to the side of the pool where I'm standing.

"I swam with a dolphin!" she says.

"I know!" My heart feels deep, ocean deep. I bend over and give her a hug. Her skin is cold, but it doesn't seem to bother her.

As Hannah swims past her, Mom leans her head against the dolphin's nose and whispers something. Maybe she's telling her a story, one about a woman who lost her memory, with no recognition of who she was or her family. One day the woman visits the beach, and right off the shore there is a pod of dolphins swimming. The woman doesn't hesitate except to take off her shoes. The waves don't bother her; when one comes toward her, she dives under it. The pod of dolphins all lift their heads. They're waiting for her, and when she swims out to where they are, they swim away together. The end.

Mom leans her head against Hannah and closes her eyes. I take a picture. I want to remember this moment, remember Mom this way.

Hannah makes a sound, and Mom echoes it. They go back and forth like this, a call-and-response exchange, for a few minutes. I wait for Mom to look me in the eyes, wait for her to say "thank you" or give me a hug—anything that tells me she knows what I've done for her.

But she doesn't. The call-and-response continues, and I start to wonder if Mom's forgotten English altogether.

"Everyone, you have a few more minutes," Beth says. "Then I need to give Hannah here some rest before our show. Are you staying to watch?"

I don't see why we can't. All we're going to do is go back to the hotel, get some food, and wait until tomorrow morning when we'll catch the bus home. "What time does the show start?" I ask.

"Starts at four o'clock and lasts for about thirty minutes."

That means it'll be about five o'clock when we leave. I'll have to call Dad before we go back to the hotel.

Mom's head is still lying against Hannah's. "You want to say goodbye?" Beth asks her.

She doesn't respond, doesn't move.

"Hannah." Beth lifts her hand in the air and waves. Hannah sticks her pectoral fin out of the water and copies Beth, waving goodbye to Mom.

But Mom still hasn't moved.

"Mom, let's take some pictures." I hold up my phone. "And then we can say goodbye to Hannah."

She kisses Hannah on the head, and I take three pictures.

"Thank you," I say to Beth. She motions for Hannah to wave goodbye to Mom one more time.

Mom moves through the water and finally gets out. She's lost some of her spark. "This is not a good place for her," she says to me.

"Who?"

"Hannah. She should be free. She should be swimming in the ocean."

I grab a towel over by the changing rooms and wrap it around Mom. "It probably would be better for her."

"It'd be better for me, too."

Maybe it would. But not for Dad. And not for me.

PUMPKIN PIE

It's the Friday before Thanksgiving break, and Bailey's sleeping over. As we ride up to the house, we see Mom's car sitting in the driveway. She's not supposed to be home yet, but I'm glad she is.

Bailey and I are laughing as we open the front door. The light is on in the kitchen, and I'm ready to say hi to Mom, but she's not there. Empty spice bottles sit on the counter next to a paper towel covered with cinnamon and nutmeg. Next to the stove, there are cans of condensed milk and pumpkin, sugar, butter, salt, and flour.

"Looks like your mom's getting ready to bake a pumpkin pie," Bailey says. "It smells good already."

"It does." I walk to the sliding glass door, seeing it's wide open. The smell of sagebrush from outside mixes with the cinnamon and nutmeg.

She's sitting in a chair under the porch awning, a sweat-shirt wrapped around her shoulders. "I can't remember your grandma's pie recipe," she says with a frown. "I can remember the ingredients just fine but not the measure-ments. I used to know them by heart."

I smile. "Well, you probably still do. I mean, I forget things all the time, like the other day when you reminded me about getting a jacket before we left for school, and then I got in the car and didn't have it."

She still seems worried, though. "I don't know if it's just everyday absentmindedness, Cassie," Mom starts to say. "I had . . ."

Bailey sticks her head out the sliding door. "Hi, Mrs. Rodrigues!"

"Hi, Bailey." Mom gets up and gives her a hug.

"You have the recipe written down somewhere?" I ask.

"I never wrote it down." Mom pushes herself up out of her chair. "I guess I should try."

Bailey and I follow Mom into the kitchen. "Maybe if we look up another recipe, it will help you remember. Aren't all pumpkin pie recipes pretty much the same?"

"For the most part, but small details make a big differ-ence." For some reason, Mom opens the utensil drawer looking for a notepad. It's an easy mistake. She must be distracted by trying to remember the recipe.

"And there's the crust," she says. "I make my own crust."

As she sits down at the table, I grab root beers for Bailey and me, and we go in the living room and watch TV. It's hard to concentrate; I hear Mom tapping a pencil, which means she's not writing anything down.

"I'll be right back," I tell Bailey.

Mom's staring outside. Blue clouds gather above the mountains. "Did you notice I was home from work early?"

"I guess I did." But I just thought she worked it out with her boss.

"I had some moments today when calculating numbers didn't make sense to me," she says.

"Maybe you were just having a bad day?" I pick up the pencil and notepad. "You tell me what to write. Will that help?"

"It was more than having a *bad day*, sweetie." She caresses my cheek. "It's been happening for a little while."

"The numbers will make sense tomorrow." They will. No one knows numbers like my mom. "You're going to be fine."

"Well, if you say so." She gets up and kisses me on the forehead.

On a shelf, above the oven, are her cookbooks. She reaches up and grabs one, then gives it to me. "We can use this."

"You don't want to try to remember?" Mom doesn't usually give up on things.

"Think it's time to start a new tradition." As she turns to the table of contents, her finger stops on *Pies*. "Page sixty-eight."

Bailey and I wash our hands at the kitchen sink. I don't like how Mom said, *It was more than having a bad day*. I'm worried. I always talk to Bailey when I'm worried, but I can't say anything right now. Behind us, Mom's gathering the rest of the ingredients—this time she opens the right cupboard the first time. Maybe I have nothing to worry about. Maybe it's just not the best day.

Bailey and I roll up our sleeves, the recipe on the counter between us.

"You ever made a pie before?" Mom asks her.

"Nope, but I've made bread with Grandma."

"Well." Mom sets a sack of sugar next to us. "If you've made bread with Lorena, you're definitely ready to make a pie." She opens the refrigerator and grabs a stick of butter.

"Look." She points to the side of the butter stick. "It shows you right on the wrapper the measurements. This is a half a cup of butter; this is a quarter cup . . ."

She takes out measuring cups and places them in a row, smallest to largest. "This is one fourth, one third, one half, and this is a cup."

I'm pretty good with measurements, converting them, too—ounces to cups, cups to pints—but I like hearing Mom give us directions. Her day is getting better.

"It's good to stick to the recipe when you're first making something." She pours water into the coffee maker.

Bailey reads the first direction out loud. "Preheat oven to four hundred twenty-five degrees."

While I turn it on, Mom's opening drawers again, the longer ones near the sink. "Here it is." She hands Bailey parchment paper. "This is for when you make the dough. I can show you how to roll and flatten it out when you're ready."

"Why don't you make the dough," Bailey says to me, "and I'll mix ingredients for the insides?"

"Sounds good."

Behind us, Mom grabs a mug, reaches for the coffeepot, and realizes it's empty. "Oh, I thought I'd started it." She fills the mug with water from the tap instead. "I'm going to be in the living room if you need me." She looks tired.

"You want me to make you some coffee?" Coffee filters and coffee are in the cupboard by the refrigerator. "You poured the water in already."

"No, that's okay." Mom walks to the living room.

Bailey scoops pumpkin into a bowl. "Your mom all right?"

"I'm not sure." I do know she'd usually be the one in the middle of whatever's going on, calling out measurements. Saying "add three teaspoons of nutmeg" or showing us her whisking technique.

"Maybe she's getting a cold or something," Bailey says.

"Yeah, maybe she is." I look down at the empty bowl where I'm supposed to mix ingredients for the dough. "I've never made piecrust before." Mom knows how. I want her here, standing beside me.

The look on her face wasn't just because she was tired. She looked lost.

Baily taps cinnamon into her mix. "I've never made a crust, either, but I'll help."

"Yeah, okay." But I don't want Bailey to help. I want Mom. "I'll be right back."

In the living room, she's sitting on the couch, staring at a blank TV screen.

I plop down next to her. "You want me to turn it on for you?"

"No." She sips some water. "I'm fine."

"Are you *fine* enough to help me make dough?" I snuggle up to her neck.

She leans her head against mine. "I'm a little tired, sweetie. You and Bailey can figure it out, can't you?"

"Please?"

"You're going to need to chill it for an hour after you make it. Once it's ready, I'll come help you roll it out, okay?"

"Okay." It's a good compromise.

"Make sure you have cold water next to you. Use it to

keep the dough moist. And wrap the dough as tight as you can."

"Got it."

She gives me another kiss, and I go back to the kitchen.

"Guess we won't be needing this yet." Bailey points to the pie filling she's mixed.

I hand her Saran wrap. "Just cover it. It should be fine."

Everything's going to be fine.

After I mix the flour, sugar, and butter, Bailey's in charge of making sure the dough doesn't get too dry. We make a good team—on the soccer field and off.

I cut the dough, and Bailey wraps one half and I wrap the other, and we set the two spheres in the refrigerator.

In the living room, Mom's fallen asleep. Maybe Bailey's right; maybe she has a cold or is getting the flu.

We have to leave the dough in the refrigerator for at least an hour, so Bailey and I go outside and kick around a soccer ball. "I need to practice my goal kicks," I tell Bailey.

"I'm the goalie, then," she says.

We're not out there for very long when Mom opens the front door and asks, "How much more time does the dough have?" Her voice has energy, like the force of the soccer ball I kick toward Bailey.

"I'll check it, okay?" Mom goes back inside.

Bailey kicks the ball back to me. "She must be feeling better."

"She just needed some rest." I dribble it toward the porch.

By the time we get to the kitchen, Mom's unsealed the dough. When she goes to grab the rolling pin, she chooses the right drawer. She holds the pin above her head like it's a club. "We're going to conquer piecrust!"

Bailey and I laugh and raise our fists. "We're ready!"

"Let's do this!" Mom sets the spheres of dough on pieces of wax paper. "I need you each to form your dough into a disk."

Once Bailey and I finish, Mom covers both disks with another piece of wax paper and presses down on the center of the dough. "Start here each time. You want to roll it out so that when you place the pie plate on top, you have about an inch of dough overlapping the edge."

Mom slides her hand under the dough and flips it onto the pie plate. She peels away the wax paper.

But then she yells, "It's starting to crack!" and the sound of her voice makes me jump. I'm not used to her yelling.

"It's cracking," she whispers this time and pushes down harder against the dough, moving fast like her life depends on her fixing all the cracks.

"Mom, it's okay." I fill a container with water. "Here. Can't we just add some . . . ?"

"The cracks are too big. Water won't help. It'll dry out.

This has never happened to me before." Mom scoops up the dough in both hands and throws it in the garbage.

I look at Bailey, wishing she could tell me what to do, what to say. "Mom, what's wrong?"

"I'm sorry," she says. "I don't know . . . I didn't mean to do that. Really. Here." She hands me the rolling pin. "You and Bailey roll out the other one. You know what to do."

Mom sits at the table and stares out the screen door. "I'm going to be okay," she says. "Don't worry. I should've kept sleeping. I'm just tired, I think." She looks up at Bailey. "When I'm tired, I get agitated very easily."

Bailey nods. "That happens to my grandma . . . and my sister. She's pretty feisty when she doesn't get enough sleep."

I don't know if the way Mom reacted was because she needs sleep, but I do know I've never seen her act like that over anything.

Bailey and I take turns rolling the dough, checking to make sure there's an inch around the edges, then flipping it onto the pie plate and peeling back the wax paper. There are some cracks this time, too, but we use the water to mend them, closing the gaps.

Bailey pours the pumpkin mix into the plate, and I put the pie in the oven and set the timer. "Twelve minutes, right?" I ask Mom.

"Yes, twelve minutes."

There's still half a bowl full of pumpkin filling left.

"We could make cookies or cake from it, couldn't we?" Bailey whispers. "I mean, I'm pretty sure we can. Why not?"

I grab the other pie plate, rub butter inside it, and pour in the rest of the filling. I open the oven door and slide in the crustless pie.

"*Why not?* is right," I say to Bailey.

"Don't worry—I've had pumpkin pie without crust before," Mom says. "It's good."

She slides open the screen. It's raining, drops tapping against the porch roof. Bailey and I follow her outside. We have about ten more minutes before the pies are done.

Mom doesn't stop under the porch. She walks to the middle of the yard, raindrops making a polka-dot pattern on her clothes. "Do you know what chaos theory is?"

"No," we both say.

"It's a theory in math about complex systems." She holds out her hand, catching a few drops. "And how one very small change in that system can have a really big impact. Pumpkin pie is simple, and so is the rain falling now. It's nice, right?"

"Yeah, it's nice." I turn toward Bailey. "Can you go check on the pies?"

"Sure," she says.

"Thanks." I take a step out in the rain and stand

shoulder to shoulder with Mom. "You're going to be okay, right?"

"Of course I am."

She would say that. She's supposed to. She's my mom.

"I'm sure once I get some sleep"—she threads her arm through mine—"I'll be fine."

She will be.

"You ever hear of the Cool Whip theory?" I ask.

"Cool Whip theory?" Mom smiles. "No."

"It studies how two big spoonfuls of Cool Whip can have a great impact on making a piece of pumpkin pie taste ten times as good—with or without the crust." I squeeze her hand, leading Mom back under the awning. "I think we should test out the theory."

"I think you're right," she says.

14

People start to fill the bleachers for the dolphin show. "Do you want to watch?" I ask Mom. "It's going to start soon."

She shrugs and goes into the changing room. When she comes out, she gives me her bathing suit and starts to walk into the bleacher area. I tie her suit to my backpack and follow her.

I don't know how long we wait. I try to get Mom to talk, but she doesn't answer any of my questions.

"How'd you like being that close to Hannah?

"What do you think she was saying when she was communicating with you?

"Was it amazing to swim with dolphins again?"

Even if she can't remember our hikes, vacations, the time we rode horses on the beach, I hope she'll be able to remember this, right now.

The show starts with music playing over a loudspeaker. Hannah and another dolphin swim across the water and do flips in the air. The crowd claps. Mom doesn't react at all. Though, why would she? This doesn't compare to what she just experienced.

Beth comes out and waves to the audience. She stands by the edge of the pool and throws each of the dolphins some fish. When she points to them and to the audience, we clap again.

When the audience claps, Hannah and another dolphin, Daisy, swim backward with the upper halves of their bodies breaching the water. Beth throws them another fish. When a set of rings is lowered over the water, Beth blows a whistle and raises her hand, and the dolphins jump through them. Then she gets in the water and swims out to the middle where Daisy and Hannah jump over her. For a last trick, Beth drapes her arms over their backs, and they carry her across the pool and back.

Beth swims to the side of the pool and gets out of the water. She waves to the audience and points to Daisy and Hannah. The audience cheers. Beth throws them some more fish.

When the show ends, Mom gets up and starts walking down the steps. I start to follow her out of the stadium, but she keeps walking straight instead of turning left.

"Mom!" I call. "Mom, what are you doing?" I start to

run and catch her arm. She's getting close to the pool. "Mom," I say, a little out of breath. I lean close and whisper in her ear, "We'll come back another time, okay? Let's go get something to eat."

"I want to stay here," she says and starts to lift one of her legs over the railing. "I want to go swim with the dolphins now."

"We'll come back," I say again. My phone's in my back pocket. It's ringing. I'm sure it's Dad. He's probably home by now. "Mom, we have to go."

Beth walks up to us. "You need some help?" she asks.

"Yeah, I think I do." I move to Mom's side. "Mom. Can you take down your foot off the railing? Let's go to the gift shop and see what they have."

Beth walks to her other side. "I don't know if this will help," she says, "but there are Hannah plushies, key chains, and posters."

Mom's still by the water, looking like she's going to climb back in. I'm not sure what would happen if she did, in her regular clothes, in front of all these people. I'm not sure I have it in me to stop her.

But then her leg slips off the railing, and she takes off toward the stadium exit. I let out a big sigh of relief and wave to Beth. "Thanks again!"

I remember when I was younger, every time we went somewhere that had a gift shop, I begged Mom and Dad to go. I liked having a memory of the day, but sometimes they had to remind me that we had to ride some rides and see some animals first.

And now, I'm here with Mom, watching her stare at a box of key chains with Hannah's picture on them, me letting her buy something to keep.

My cell phone starts ringing again. I can't avoid this forever.

"Hi, Dad."

"Cassie! Why didn't you answer at home? I told you to come home. Are you still at Bailey's?"

"We're . . . in San Diego."

"San Diego? What?"

"Yes, I took Mom to the aquatic center. She swam with dolphins, just like she wanted."

Dad pauses. I know he's mad. "I can't believe you lied to me. I was worried."

"Dad . . . I know it was wrong, but I did it for a good reason."

That wasn't a good thing to say.

"We're going to talk about this more, but I need you to stay right where you are. I'm coming to get you."

"It's a long drive, Dad." I tell him we have bus tickets home tomorrow morning, and we're going to stay in the hotel tonight, and it'll be fine.

"Bailey is going to bring some bikes to us, and we're going to ride home from the bus station. It only takes fifteen minutes."

I'm trying to not burden him. This trip was my idea, and I want to do it from beginning to end by myself.

There's silence on the other end of the line, and I think maybe there's a chance he's going to agree. Or maybe he's getting ready to yell.

Looking over at Mom, sitting across from me in the back seat of a taxi, I try not to think how mad Dad is, how I disappointed him. I made Mom's life, her existence with this disease, better. It's all I can do.

If I get in trouble when we get back, even if she forgets what she did today, it doesn't matter. We made it here. We did it. I did it, for Mom.

But instead, he sighs. "You didn't have to lie to me, Cassie."

Our last conversation comes rushing back to me, and I start to cry. "I did. Because you'd already decided you didn't want to take Mom. I asked you. I gave you a chance."

"Cassie, I'm sorry. Just give me the name of the hotel. We can talk about it later."

I don't want to argue anymore, either.

When we get to the hotel, I check in. I don't have much food left, but I dump what I do have onto a table. For dinner, I let Mom have the peanut butter and jelly sandwiches, and I take the crackers. While eating her second sandwich, Mom stands by the window, looking down at a swimming pool. "I want to go swim."

Her suit is still wet, but she doesn't care. I help her put it on, and we walk down to the pool. No one else is inside the gated area. On the fence, one of the signs says POOL HOURS 9 AM TO 8 PM. I check my phone. We have some time.

Mom doesn't hesitate and dives into the water. The stuffed Hannah we bought at the gift shop dives in with her. I stand by the edge and watch her, a red and orange blur. She lingers at the bottom a little while. I wonder if she's waiting for more dolphins to join her.

At seven fifty-two, Mom's still in the water. She swims back and forth, from one end to the other, sometimes diving down and touching the bottom. Stuffed Hannah is lying on the side of the pool now.

When she swims to the side, I dip my hand into the water to get her attention. "Mom, it's time to get out."

She takes a breath but then waves and pushes off the pool wall, ignoring me. She's been swimming for an hour.

All of a sudden, I realize I don't want her to ever get

out of the water. I don't want to take her home with me, because she needs this. I need this. The memory of Mom swimming, with or without the dolphins. She'll be infinite, going on and on and on.

Maybe Dad was right. Maybe I shouldn't have brought her. Now that she swam with dolphins, what else is there to do? Back home, she'll be sitting in a chair all day, eating cheese and crackers, just watching images on TV. Moving to High Desert Village. It feels like the end of her story.

But it's getting late. I stick my hand into the water again, this time catching her ankle as she pushes off the side. "Mom, it's time to get out."

She pulls away from me and keeps swimming. I take off my shoes and stick my feet in the water.

I look toward the parking lot for headlights. Dad should be here soon. I don't see him, but I hear footsteps behind me.

"Excuse me." A girl wearing a shirt with the hotel logo stands by the gate. "The swimming pool is closed now. It'll open back up tomorrow morning."

"Uh, okay . . . thanks."

The girl leaves. I wait for Mom to swim to the side again, but she's hanging out in the deep end. "Mom! It's time to get out."

She sinks into the water. At first I think she's going to swim toward me, but when she comes up for air, she's in the middle of the pool, out of reach. She's not coming out.

I slide into the water, waist deep, the water colder than I thought. No wonder Mom keeps moving.

I wait for her to swim to my end, but she doesn't. The pool light turns her into a blurry silhouette, and she dives under.

She stays underwater for at least a minute, breaks the surface, and takes a deep breath; then she dives back down. I count how long it takes her to come up for air and wonder if she's building her lung capacity, preparing herself for her journey.

I take a breath. The water is cold, especially at the bottom. I imagine that Mom has skin cells like a sea mammal's, a thick epidermis. I imagine that when she was born, she was round and pudgy, her body ready for the cold. She had to shed the layer of blubber she was born with in order to survive the warmer climate. But cells have memory.

It takes a second for me to adjust my eyes, but I find the reddish orange of Mom's swimsuit. I am not as good of a swimmer as she is, not as fast, but I don't realize how fast she is until I'm in the water with her. I don't know if I've ever actually swam with Mom, not side by side.

She moves like a dolphin, holding her arms straight in front of her, her hips and legs moving up and down.

I reach out to touch her heel. The bottoms of her feet are white, almost like a ghost.

She'll eventually get tired. She'll eventually get hungry. Or maybe she'll start to grow a dorsal fin right before my eyes. Maybe her skin cells, after being submerged in the cold for a long period of time, will remember what she was.

I see her head breaking the surface, blowing a spray of water into the air. I dive down again. I'm going to need a little luck in order to catch her. But I know I have to get her out.

I swim as fast as I can, but she's faster, swimming back and forth, going from the bottom to the surface at least ten times.

I'm tired. I grab on to the side and lean my head against my hands. Lifting myself out of the water, I feel the weight of my clothes, heavy against my skin.

I'm not sure what to do. I lean back on my hands and stare through the fence, out to the parking lot. Dad's car is white. It would glow like Mom's feet. But I don't see it yet.

I take a deep breath and jump back in the water, diving deep, bubbles passing behind me.

Using my legs to thrust me through the water, I search for a glimpse of her. I see the bottoms of Mom's feet like two rectangular moons, shining in the blue, and reach for one. I reach as hard and as far as possible, and I manage to grab her ankle again, but it doesn't seem to stop her one bit. She keeps swimming, pulling me along with her. I try to stop. I try to lean backward. I'm running out of breath.

I manage to grab her ankle with my other hand, and with the breath I have left, I yank. I'm not letting her go. I don't want her to go.

I start to cry. My tears blend with the water. "Mom," I scream, "I'm not going to let you go! I need you to stay!"

And then she stops resisting and floats, letting her arms hang down. I don't know if she heard me yelling, but as she brings up her head, she takes a breath.

Somewhere inside her, even though it's hidden away, she has to know I still need her.

I wait for her to say my name. "Mom," I whisper. We're both holding on to the side. "You know me. Cassie. I'm Cassie."

For a split second, her eyes don't hold that faraway look in them.

"Cassie," I whisper again. But she just looks away.

The gate opens and closes. Dad's standing by one of the patio chairs, holding a towel. He helps Mom get out first.

I wait in the water, trying to stop crying. Snot is dripping out of my nose.

"Cassie." Dad's holding a towel for me, too.

"I'm sorry."

"I know. It's time to get out."

He wraps me in the towel, and we walk over to Mom, now lying on one of the lounge chairs. I lie down next to her and listen to the rhythm of her breathing. It's slow, steady. I try to breathe, too.

15

Dad buys bags of chips and trail mix from a vending machine, and we go up to the room to eat them.

He tries to get Mom to take a shower, to warm up, but instead she opens a bag of Lay's and eats three at a time.

When I come out of the shower, he's bought five more bags of chips. "Your mom's hungry." I realize I didn't have much for dinner.

I take a bag of Doritos and grab my phone. "Look," I say. I sit down next to Mom and show them the pictures I took with Hannah and her.

Some are just blurry images of her swimming under the surface. One shows Mom's and Hannah's heads sticking out of the water. They're both smiling (or it looks like Hannah is, anyway).

"It looks like fun," Mom says. "I swam a lot." She reaches behind her for another bag of chips.

The memory of today is somewhere inside her, but it's unreachable. In a weird way, this makes me feel better about her forgetting my name. Even something this amazing might not stick with her.

The next picture, the last one I took, is my favorite. I took it by accident. Most of the photograph shows the water, but at the very top is Mom's hand breaching the surface in one corner, and the edge of Hannah's fin in the other. It's a photograph of motion, of moving forward, of being part of this world but not part of it at the same time.

In many ways, it reminds me of living with Mom now. The world passes by, but then there's this person I love with a disease that makes the world slow down. I want to keep going forward as fast as possible, passing the hard parts, but I also want to keep everything still before it goes away.

I remember thinking when Mom got sick that I was going to try to make every moment with her count, but it's been hard. I think I did the best I could.

"Did I keep up?" Mom asks. "Was I able to keep up with the dolphin when we swam together?"

"You were amazing."

"That's good."

After Mom's eaten about five or six bags of chips, she takes a shower.

Dad sits down on the edge of the bed. "Desert Village called this morning. The assisted-living place. They'll have an opening in the fall. I'm going to go and see one of the rooms next week."

"I don't know if I want to come with you." There are just crumbs left at the bottom of the Doritos bag.

"You don't have to."

"I feel like I should, though. It's supposed to be nice, right?"

"That's what I've heard."

"They'll take good care of Mom?"

"They better."

"What happens if they don't?"

Dad opens the bathroom door to check on Mom. "Then, we bring her back."

"It's going to be different without her living at home."

"I know." Dad sits on the floor next to me.

"I had to bring her here." I pick up Mom's Hannah plushie she left on the floor. It's still wet.

Dad holds out his hand, and I give him the stuffed animal. "Moving her to Desert Village—well, I'm thinking of her safety and . . . I'm thinking of us. It sounds selfish, but Mom's not going to . . ."

"Get any better?"

"Right, and . . ."

"It's going to get harder and harder for us to take care of her."

Dad holds Hannah against his heart. "I should've said yes. I should've come with you today." He leans over and kisses me on the forehead. "I'm glad you brought her. I'm also relieved that everything went okay."

Dad gives me Hannah and helps Mom out of the shower. I turn on the TV and find a nature show. It's about the rain forest. In her pajamas, Mom lies in bed, and she and Dad fall asleep to macaws flying tree to tree.

I find my sketch pad in my backpack. I open to a blank page and draw.

Mom still hasn't said my name. I was hoping the joy of swimming with dolphins would be overwhelming enough to trigger a connection, somewhere in her memories, to remember "Cassie."

I pick up my phone and look at the pictures again.

No matter how much a memory fades, it's still somewhere deep in Mom's brain. No matter how much she forgets, it's still a part of her. That means me, too. I'm still with her. I just need to keep reminding myself of that.

———

When we get home the next morning, I go to my room and take out the stack of photographs I found in Mom's collection. I go through them, choosing the ones I want to use, and print out one from San Diego.

In the middle of a new collage, I'm going to glue the photograph. It'll represent what our life is now.

I scan more photos and start cutting. There are slivers of images everywhere, and I go through two cylinders of glue, cutting memories into pieces.

I hold the collage in front of Mom.

She presses her finger against the pictures. I wait. Her eyes move from me to the close-ups.

Please say my name. Cassie. It's Cassie.

But it's lost, and no matter how hard she tries, she can't find it. I tried. Decomposing memories isn't going to help, either.

Mom leans to the side. I'm blocking her view of the TV. I sigh and go back to my room.

———

I lay the collage flat on the floor, and before pushing it under my bed, I catch a glimpse of one of the photographs. It's of my foot, making contact with a soccer ball.

Bailey. I forgot about her. She must have been waiting at the bus station with the bikes. I didn't let her know the plan changed.

I grab my backpack and start running out the door and

down the sidewalk. "I'm going to Bailey's!" I yell to Dad, who glances up out of the hood of his car. "I won't be long."

I make a quick stop at a food mart and buy two bags of Takis, chili lime flavored.

When I get to Bailey's house, I jump over our two bikes lying on the porch. I knock and hold up the Takis so they're the first thing Bailey sees when she opens the door.

But Grandma Lorena answers. "Hello, Cassandra. Come in," she says. As I follow her, she walks straight to the kitchen to make me something to eat.

"Grandma Lorena, I'm not hungry."

"Not even a piece of zucchini bread? I made it this morning."

"No, thank you. I just need to talk to Bailey."

"She's been in her room all day, moping around. Not like her. Maybe you can get her to go outside for some fresh air, huh?"

"Maybe."

Grandma Lorena opens Bailey's door. "Someone's here to see you."

"If it's Cassie, tell her she can go home and I'll talk to her at school."

Grandma Lorena steps back into the hallway with me. "Wait here, dear."

She walks into Bailey's room, and I hear her talking in

Spanish. I don't understand what she's saying, but it sounds like she's trying to get Bailey to talk to me.

The door opens. "You can go in, Cassie."

Bailey's sitting on her bed, throwing a ball up in the air, her back turned toward me. "If you came to get your bike . . ."

"No, I came to say thanks . . . for helping me get to the bus station. And sorry for not showing up when I said we would." I sit down on the other side of the bed. "Mom swam with a dolphin, and my dad came to pick us up."

Bailey looks at me. She's been crying. "I waited for you. I even went inside to ask if the bus was late, if it'd broken down. Then the bus showed up and you weren't on it."

"I forgot to call you and tell you . . ."

"You can't do that. You can't forget me. Not again." Bailey misses the ball, and it rolls against the wall. "I know your mom's sick and it's sad and I'm—"

"No, you're right." I pick up the soccer ball and toss it to her. "Here, I brought you these." I set the bags of Takis on the bed. "Thanks for being there for me, Bailey. I hope you can forgive me. I promise to be a better friend."

I close the bedroom door as softly as I can and say goodbye to Grandma Lorena.

"Wait," she says and gives me a loaf of zucchini bread to take home.

Riding back, I follow the white shoulder line painted on the road.

On Monday, I wouldn't blame Bailey if the circle she usually stands in with Nathan, Marissa, and Diana doesn't include me, if I'm not part of their 360 degrees.

16

I decide to visit High Desert Village with Mom and Dad after all. The place Mom will live is like an apartment. It has a bedroom, a small living room, and a bathroom. In the back, it has a small porch area with a tall wooden fence around it. There are doctors and nurses who will be there to help her. The apartment comes furnished, so there's already a couch and a chair in the living room.

I hear Dad ask Mom, "Do you like it?" He pauses to give her time to nod or to communicate whatever answer she'd like to give. One thing that's always been true about Dad, even when Mom wasn't sick, is he always waits to give his opinion until after she's given hers.

But ultimately this isn't Mom's decision to make; it's Dad's. Though I think he's hoping that if she says yes, the weight of his making the decision won't be so heavy.

I sit down on a small, hard couch. Maybe we can get Mom a new one that's more like the one in our living room. I'm probably going to have to help Dad pack up some of Mom's things, but everything she owns won't fit in here.

Her ceramic glass dolphins will, the ones I've glued so far. I'll look at each one of them close up before wrapping them in paper. I'll see where each of their cracks are, the lines where I've glued them back together.

The day we move her, a couple of suitcases will be by the door. I'll take one to the car. That morning, every detail will be important. More important than they have been for the last year.

I know my heart will feel wide and deep and heavy.

As we leave, I'll kiss Mom on the cheek. She might not respond. I'll feel bad about wanting her to say my name one more time. I'll close my eyes and try to remember the sound of her saying it and wonder if, when she tries to remember the sound of my name, the vibration of it blends with her memory of the vibration of dolphins. I'd like to think that it does, that those sounds come together and are one. "I love you," I'll whisper. Maybe the sound of that, too, and the sound of Dad's name, and his saying, "I love you," will stay with her. We'll promise to visit all the time.

Now Dad turns to me. "This is okay. It's nice, right?" he asks. He leans his arm on my shoulders. "It's small. Cozy."

"Yeah, I guess it's fine."

Mom sits next to me, and I hold her hand.

When we get into the car, Dad turns down the music. "It's the best thing to do, right?" I'm not sure if he's talking to me or himself. I want to say that Mom staying at home is the right thing, because if we put her in this place, it'll feel like we're abandoning her. "I'm not sure."

"Yeah," he says. He pulls the car over to the side of the road and stares out the front window. "I don't know what to do."

Then something catches Mom's eye out of the window. "A swimming pool!" she yells. She's pointing to three plastic pools that are sitting outside a Walgreens. "I want one of those."

Dad seems to think for a minute, and then he turns the car around and pulls into a parking space.

There are boxes of blow-up swimming pools stacked outside the front doors. Dad grabs one and goes to the register. "Follow your mom," he says.

She's wandering down the aisle that has electronic gadgets, toys, and things that are advertised on TV.

There are puzzles, too. She picks up a box that has an autumn scene. "Thanksgiving's coming. We have to get a turkey," she says.

"Thanksgiving isn't for a while, so we have plenty of time to get a turkey."

"Are you going to make stuffing?" Mom asks. "The stuffing is always the best part."

"I don't know how to make it. But you tried to teach me how to make a pie." That seems to satisfy her.

In the next aisle, Mom grabs a bag of black licorice, a box of Red Hots, and some peppermint Life Savers. "The turkey has to be the right size. It won't fit in the oven if it's too big."

"Ten pounds, right?"

"Yeah, and green beans. I just warm them up from a can."

"Cassie?" Dad says from the front of the store.

I take the candy from her and give it to Dad. The doors open, and Mom heads outside.

"Cassie." Dad throws me the car keys and gets on line.

Outside the store, Mom watches a little girl ride on a miniature merry-go-round. The music coming from the ride sounds warped and gooey, but the little girl smiles as she goes around and around, riding a pink horse.

"Mom, I have the keys if you want to go to the car."

Once we're in, we wait for Dad. Mom says, "Getting the right size turkey is important. You should know that. There'll be leftovers. For sandwiches. Mayonnaise and turkey on yours. You need to make sure your dad takes the time to pick out just the right one."

I know we just came from the care center and that this

might be true. But I don't like when she talks like this, like there will be a time in the very near future when she doesn't exist. She makes it seem so normal, like she's saying in her own way, "Look, Cassie, this is what's coming. Get used to it. If you do, it will be easier when it happens."

It's not going to be easier. I'm losing her, and it's going to be really hard.

I climb over the seat and sit by her. Mom places her hand on my leg and leans to the side. She looks up through the front windshield. The moon is faded in the afternoon sky. Across the street is the open desert. Mom stares at it with me.

It's quiet, and I don't feel like crying, so I start humming "Girls Just Want to Have Fun." The humming turns into singing. I sing the words just above a whisper, and Mom sings, too.

The trunk popping open signals Dad is back. I jump out of the car and help slide the swimming pool box inside. Mom is still singing, or it's the reverberation of her singing that I still hear, the sound hitting the mountains a mile away from here and bouncing back, loud and clear.

"Everything okay?" Dad asks.

"Yeah, I guess."

The okay things at this moment: Mom still remembers how many pounds a turkey has to weigh in order to fit in our oven. She still remembers what I like on my turkey sandwiches. And she remembers the words to "Girls Just Want to Have Fun."

———————

I'm sitting in the inflated swimming pool. Dad and I set it up under the porch in our backyard. Mom's across from me, both of us in our swimsuits. We're pushing a rubber dolphin back and forth to each other. The dolphin skims the water. Sometimes it runs into Mom's toe. The water's cool.

The sun is still warm, and even though it's dinnertime, we're having breakfast. There are orange juice and bagels on the table. Dad's sitting with us, too, in a beach chair. The look on his face is one I see often now, one of relaxation and relief but a little bit of sadness, of finally being able to let go of trying to hold everything together, of letting pieces fall where they may.

I know if it were Mom's choice, she would write *Cassie* with the tip of her finger across the sky every morning.

I push the rubber dolphin across the water, and she pushes it back to me. Dad is eating a bagel, and it's quiet except for the faint sound of low, happy music coming from down the street.

Dolphins, Mom told me, even years and years after

they're separated from their pod, can remember one another's sounds. Cousins can identify cousins, children can recognize parents, parents know their children. All by the smallest fraction of sound.

I fill the rubber dolphin with water and squeeze it. Water squirts out of the dolphin's blowhole. Mom grabs it and fills it again.

I remember when the doctor told Dad and me that there was no cure for Alzheimer's, that there were ways for them to slow it down, but the effects of the disease were inevitable.

I'd looked up the word "inevitable." It means "certain to happen, unavoidable." It meant there wasn't anything we could do.

But Mom has taught me there is always a way, no matter how small, to make things better.

When she does move to High Desert Village, and we leave her there, the hardest part will be coming home. We'll walk through the house, going from room to room, and not ever be able to find what's gone.

We'll turn on the TV because the house will be too quiet. We'll turn it on just to have something to listen to, just as a reminder, just to have a piece of normal.

The sound of Mom not being here will get to be the new normal. I'll try to replace the sound with new sounds, or I'll try to think about math, about the endless values of decimals, but I'll know that memories, even though I always thought they were endless, too, have an end for some people.

I'll think of Mom, think of how she's probably sitting in her apartment in High Desert Village, eating food that they've brought her, watching TV, and hope she thinks she's at home, or that she's thinking of mountaintops, or of the ocean because the ocean's capacity is deep and wide, like the desert, like the heart, like the memories I have of her.

Mom pushes the dolphin across the water. I cradle it in my hand for a second before pushing it back to her.

17

That night, the sound of the front door opening wakes me up.

Mom's standing at the edge of the yard, her arms folded across her chest, staring at the mountains. The night is cold and clear. The stars look close enough to pick out of the sky. "We never hiked to the top, did we?" Mom asks.

"We can do it tomorrow," I say, because why not?

"We could. There's a trail to the top. We'd have to leave early."

Dad comes up behind me. The door opening must have woken him up, too. To my surprise, he says, "I can take you to the trailhead."

"You don't have to work tomorrow, right?" I ask.

"No," he says. "Let's go."

Mom twists her hands through my and Dad's arms,

and we look at the mountain we're going to climb tomorrow. In some ways, I feel like I've already climbed a mountain.

"Mom . . . ," I start. I want to tell her that because of her, I'm so much braver. That even though she can't remember everything she taught me, I can. That six months ago, I would never have been able to travel on a bus without Dad's permission. To be the one who helped check the dream off her list. But the words get stuck.

"What do you think you want to take with us to eat tomorrow?" I ask instead. It's enough for now.

——————

The day's cold, and there's a breeze blowing. From the trailhead, gray clouds reach out over the valley. Mom starts to ask a lot of questions, whether we have enough food, water, whether we'd turned off all the lights in the house before we left.

When she first got sick, Dad thought that she was being paranoid. Now, on the trailhead, he just answers her questions and comforts her.

At the midway point, Mom stops and looks out over the valley. "Do you see that?" she asks us and points out to the desert floor. "Do you see the ocean?"

"Ocean?" Dad says. "What do you see, Kim?"

"Water," she answers. "Isn't it beautiful?"

Dad just stares out across the desert, too. "Yes, it is," he says. "Yes, it's beautiful."

We don't make it to the peak. Three-quarters of the way up the trail, Mom turns around again and says she wants to go home. So we turn around and go back.

At the house, Mom doesn't take off her jacket or her hiking boots. She sits right down in her chair and turns on the TV. It wasn't one of her good days.

———————

The deadline to enter the art show passes. The following Tuesday, our class gets a sneak peek. We walk to the building across the street from school, where it's set up.

Mrs. G points to a blue curtain. "We'll reveal the mural during open house."

Most of the student art pieces are sketches or paintings, some in watercolor. Some are flowers, some are self-portraits, some are landscapes. One is a field of sunflowers with a red barn in the background.

Bailey's at the end of the line. From the corner of my eye, I can see her waving her hand to get my attention.

Where's yours? she mouths.

I shake my head.

At recess, she finds me sitting on a bench with my

sketchbook and some sunflower seeds. I crack a seed and put the shell in my pocket.

"So where's your art piece?" Bailey's fingertips are red, covered in chili lime flavoring.

I'm surprised she's talking to me at all. "Thought you were mad at me."

"I am. But you're changing the subject."

"You're not playing soccer today?"

Bailey crumples up her Taki bag. "You're changing the subject again. Did Mrs. G forget to point out your art? Did I miss it?"

"No."

"So . . ."

"She didn't forget. You didn't miss it."

"You didn't enter?"

"No."

"Why not?"

From my other pocket, I grab more seeds and shove them into my mouth. I owe Bailey some kind of answer. "I wasn't inspired."

"Really?"

"Yes, *really*." I spit the shells into my hand this time and walk to the garbage. It's a good excuse to try and escape her questions.

"You're supposed to be mad at me," I remind her again.

"I can be mad and still ask why you don't have anything in the art show."

I throw the shells into the garbage can. "Okay. I made something, but it . . . it didn't help my mom. And focusing on my mom made me forget about you. So I just want to leave it where it is."

She seems like she wants to ask more, but she lets me continue.

"Bailey . . . I'm really sorry I forgot to tell you about not coming to the bus station. I'm sorry about a lot of things, like my mom getting sick and me not being a good friend . . ."

"You've already apologized. I believe you."

The bell rings. When we line up, Bailey and I are both at the back of the line. She crunches Takis until Mrs. G tells her to put them away.

"If you made something, you should put it in the art show."

I tell her I'll think about it.

———————

At the after-school program, between math problems, I take out my plastic dolphin bottle and move it side to side. My name, written on the dolphins' flukes, moves with the motion, too.

I do the next problem. We're back to multiplication, the math operation that Mrs. G told us reminds her of the word "possibilities."

I look up from doing math, and Bailey's standing in the doorway. I drop my pencil. "Why are you here?"

She ignores my question and reaches behind her. She's holding my collage. "Mrs. Collins let me in. I figured you probably put it under your bed, where you put your mom's self-portrait."

"The deadline was last Friday," I say.

"It's worth a try to see if they'll still take it. I can ask."

"Why are you doing this?" I know she said she accepted my apology, but I let her down.

"Because you're my friend, and friends help each other out," she says. Then she adds with a smile, "Plus, I'm getting tired of riding my bike alone on Saturdays."

The only thing left to say is "thank you."

The night of open house, there's a knock on our door. It's Mrs. Collins.

"Did you forget something?" I ask.

"No." She sets her purse in the regular spot. "I'm here to stay with your mom until you get back."

Oh. "I thought she was going with us."

"I don't know, sweetie. Your dad just asked me if I could come back and stay with her." Mrs. Collins usually doesn't give her opinion; she says her job is just to take care of whatever needs to be cleaned up or anything Mom needs.

But she can tell I'm sad. She places her hand on my shoulder. "Maybe talk to your dad?"

When Dad comes out into the living room, I tell him I really want Mom to go with us. I guess I shouldn't be surprised when he says he doesn't think it would be a good place for her to be, "In case she makes a scene."

"Then, we'll leave. I want her to come."

Dad's going to try to convince me that Mom should stay here, but I'm prepared to play the what-if game. "I want her to go. It might be the last . . ."

He gets a sad look in his eyes, and I feel bad for saying it. But I think it worked. "Okay," he says. "Mrs. Collins, I'm sorry you went through the trouble of driving back here."

Mrs. Collins grabs her purse and goes to the door. "It's okay. Don't worry. Kim should go."

Dad takes Mom to the bedroom to change her clothes. She comes wearing her favorite red dress. She looks beautiful.

We visit my classroom first. Dad looks through the work on my desk, and I show him and Mom some computer projects I did on my Chromebook. Mom stares at the screen for a few minutes, then wanders through the desks and around the classroom. She stops at the Revolutionary War projects on the back counters and tables.

Dad follows her and is soon joined by Mrs. G. "Hello, Mr. Rodrigues." She shakes my dad's hand. "And hello, Mrs. Rodrigues," she says, gesturing at Mom. "So glad you both could come tonight." There's a weird quiet. I can tell Mrs. G isn't sure how to react to Mom not saying hello back, not shaking her hand.

"Mrs. G," I say, "it's okay. She does that to us sometimes, too."

She places her arms around my shoulders and bends down. "Thank you for telling me that," she whispers.

"No problem."

As she turns to go greet other parents, Dad tells her to wait for a moment. "Cassie's told me how much she loves your class," he tells her.

"It's a pleasure to have her," Mrs. G says.

I spot Bailey coming in through the back door with Grandma Lorena and Sonia in tow. They all come up to say hello, then Grandma Lorena looks around and finds Mom staring at the poetry hanging on the white board.

"Kim," she says and gives Mom a hug. I hold my breath. I'm not sure how Mom's going to react to Grandma Lorena hugging her. I'm not sure she'll remember who she is.

But Mom smiles, and Grandma Lorena talks to her the way she always used to. "I'm going to bring you some soup and some tortillas. I've been meaning to do that for a long time, but you know how time slips away from us . . ."

She pauses and looks over at Dad. "I'm sorry; I didn't mean to say . . ."

"It's fine," Dad says, "and we'd love some of your soup."

Bailey nudges me. "Have you been to the art show yet? What'd your mom and dad think? When my grandma saw your work, she said, 'Cassandra has bared her soul in this. That's what good art does.'"

I smile. "Your grandma's art is cooking. She bares her soul in a pot of beans." Now Bailey smiles.

I tell her we haven't gone over yet. I'm a little nervous.

"The mural came out pretty good, too," Bailey says. "Everyone's piece is different, but the colors and images connect to one another."

"Guess that was Mrs. G's goal, huh?"

"Definitely."

Mom, Dad, and I say goodbye, and we walk across the street to the art show.

"Here it is." I stand to the side of my piece. "What do you think?" Which is a silly thing to ask, because Dad always tells me.

He's silent for a moment. He reads the title: *The Space Between Lost and Found.*

He leans forward, focusing on the center photograph. "It's your mom, swimming."

His eyes start in the middle, then look at the photographs that surround the blurred version of Mom. Then out to pieces of images of us as a family and then to Mom when she was young. Just as I planned.

"It's beautiful, Cassie," Dad says. "Different than what you've done before. Still has depth, but it has—at least for me—more layers of emotion. It's more realistic, but it also has a dreamlike quality to it. It's really something."

Mom moves to another watercolor, this one abstract. The title is *Blue Tornado.* The paper is covered with wisps of swirling blue brushstrokes. "Lots of movement," Dad says.

Then he goes back over and stands in front of my collage. "I think we should hang this by Mom's portrait in the living room. What do you think?"

"I think we'll have to get another frame for Mom's portrait before we do that. It broke."

Now Mom's looking over my shoulder at the collage.

She steps around me and reaches up, like she did at home, and caresses the blurred photograph.

Her eyes follow the path of images. I wait. I wait for her to say, "Cassie."

Part of me was expecting the collage to be a final magic wand. *Abracadabra. Poof.* All of a sudden, pieces would slide back into Mom's brains cells, connecting bit by bit until she remembered.

But the pieces aren't enough, not anymore.

"That's you." I point to the blurred image. "Swimming."

I point to some of the other photographs, telling her about them, telling her about where we were and what we were doing. "This is the campfire we built on the beach. It was our first trip to the ocean. This is when we went to Disneyland and you said, 'We can't come all the way to Disneyland, buy a Mickey Mouse hat, and not get our names sewn on.' This is when we hiked the Black Desert Trail, a ten-mile hike." And, "That's a trophy you won when you were my age. You were an amazing swimmer."

"She still is." Dad's voice breaks a little. "We took some great trips."

"We did," I say. "We still can," I whisper. But this time I'm not sure I believe it.

The last thing we do before we leave the art show is

look at the mural. In the middle of my saguaro cactus is a lone elf owl. On her half, Bailey's drawn saguaro cacti, too, except hers are small. Everything does blend well together. The other panels show desert landscapes with desert animals, but in the middle of the mural is a panel where someone's drawn our school and part of our town. The colors are a balance of cool and warm.

If I'd drawn an ocean scene, it would've been one part disconnected from the whole. This is better.

When we get home, Dad turns off the ignition, and Mom opens the car door. She takes off down the sidewalk. It's dark out, only a crescent moon in the sky, but streetlights shine, casting silhouettes on the ground.

"The house is this way," Dad says and gently grabs her arm.

But Mom pulls away. "We're going on a trip."

We follow her to where the roads ends and where the desert starts. She still doesn't stop.

"It's too dark, Kim. We'll come out here tomorrow."

"We used to go on trips," Mom says. I wonder if she overheard me before.

Dad walks right beside her, looking on the ground, making sure her path is clear so she doesn't trip over anything. The sagebrush where I hid the folding chairs is lit by the moon.

"The canyon is up ahead." Mom takes off her shoes but leaves on her socks. Lying down on the desert floor, she spreads her arms out to the sides and makes a sand angel. Dad seems to think of stopping her, telling her to get up, but he doesn't. He lays down right beside her and mimics her movements, and when she stops, he holds her hand, and they close their eyes.

I sit down and rest my chin on my knees. Out here, the canyon swallows sound and turns it into an echo.

The sky is a dark, dark purple, and stars shine. The echo of the river at the bottom of the canyon carries up through the space and rocks, the movement of water sounding almost like voices. But other than that, it's quiet.

Since Mom got sick, I've tried to imagine what the house will feel like once she's not there. It's impossible.

I think of the desert, the sand, and how right now it's breaking down to the smallest of particles. We don't notice because it takes so long and there is so much.

Dad sits up, leans back on his hands, and stares out toward the canyon. "It's beautiful out here."

"And it's in our backyard."

"It is," Dad says and smiles.

If I had to draw a sketch to end our story together, it would be just this. The three of us, lying on the desert floor at the edge of a canyon, holding hands, the stars doing what they've done for millions of years, infinitely shining.

18

Saturday morning, I'm in my room. On my desk are sticks, pieces of erasers, broken pencils, a couple of bottle caps. They're pieces that used to belong to something bigger that I'm transforming into something new. And I still have the rest of Mom's dolphins to glue together.

There's a knock on the front door. It's Mrs. Collins. "Good morning, Cassie."

"Mrs. Collins, it's Saturday." I'm wearing my soccer shorts and shirt, dressed for a day with Bailey.

"I know, but . . ." She goes to the kitchen.

"But what?"

"Talk to your dad."

I turn around. "Dad?"

We meet each other in the middle of the hallway. Before I can ask, he says, "Why are you wearing your soccer uniform?"

"Bailey and I are going to the park today."

"Oh, well, I have a surprise for you." I follow him back out to the living room.

Mom walks in, holding a plate of Ritz crackers with cheese. I kiss her on the cheek as she passes me on her way to her chair.

"I don't want to tell you what it is," Dad says, "but it's going to take most of the day, and don't eat breakfast, okay? Bailey's welcome to join us if she wants."

He goes outside. I lift the blinds and watch, to see if I can figure out where we're going. He opens the hood of the car and checks the oil. That was his routine when we used to go on road trips.

I dial Bailey's number. Grandma Lorena answers. As soon as I say hello, she says, "I'll get Miss Bailey . . ."

"Hi, Cassie."

"I know we had plans to go to the park today, but my dad has some sort of surprise. He says it'll take most of the day. Do you want to come with us?"

"Sure, I love surprises," she says.

"Can you be ready in half an hour?"

"Let me ask my grandma." Grandma Lorena thinks it's a great idea.

Bailey and I hang up, and Dad walks through the door. He kisses Mom and finds Mrs. Collins. "We should be back around five," I hear him say. "Thank you so much."

He pats his jeans to check for his wallet. "You ready?"

"I guess. Am I?"

The sun is shining as we pull out of the driveway. It's always a good time to look at the mountains, but the best is times like now, when they're a deep shade of blue and purple.

We pick up Bailey, and then Dad drives to the Donut Shop. "Thought we'd get some maple bars first. And I don't think any ice-cream shops are open this early." Dad turns to Bailey. "Do you like maple bars?"

"I like any kind of doughnut," Bailey says.

Inside the shop, Dad orders a half dozen. "You can't eat all of them yourself, Cassie. You have to share with Bailey and me," he teases.

Mom loves maple bars, too. As I watch the guy behind the counter place the doughnuts into a pink box, I remember when I tasted them for the first time. I thought they looked too gross to eat, but Mom said, "They're doughnuts. Do doughnuts ever taste bad?" and tore off a bite for me. "If you never eat a maple bar, you're going to miss out on one of the most amazing tastes in the world."

I take a deep breath to hold back tears. I think about my collage. Dad said we could hang it in the living room, but I think the best place for it will be in Mom's apartment at High Desert Village. Even if she doesn't remember swimming with the dolphins, doesn't remember our trips together, she'll be happy when she looks at it, and that is something. I made it for her. I made it to try to help her remember. It didn't work. But it's still beautiful.

"You two ready to go?" Dad asks.

In the car, he sets the pink box between Bailey and me and gives me a handful of napkins. "Dig in."

As we drive toward the highway, Dad turns on the radio. It's the news.

I tear a piece of maple bar like Mom did for me the first time I tasted one, and it sticks to my finger. I take a bite and it is one of the best-tasting things ever.

"Think we need some music," Dad says. He changes the radio to an eighties station. I don't know the song that's playing now, but he does. He starts to hum, which I haven't heard him do in a long time.

Bailey and I laugh.

The next song that plays is a Cyndi Lauper one. It's not "Girls Just Want to Have Fun" but another song, "Time After Time." It's on the same album, and I remember Mom playing the song over and over, too, and singing it just as loud.

So that's what we do. We remember. And we sing.

ACKNOWLEDGMENTS

Writing this book was cathartic for me. When my father suffered from Alzheimer's, my mom was his primary caretaker for a long time. She worked a full-time job, took care of him, and was still supportive of her children and her grandchildren. There came a point in my father's disease where she had to make some difficult decisions, and I'm grateful we—my brothers, sister, sisters-in-law, nieces, and nephews—were able to come together and support her. In those difficult moments, we shared our fears and vulnerabilities, but we were there for each other. This is a testament to both my parents.

Showing up, staying, and working through the difficult parts—all are strong themes of my acknowledgments to those who supported me in writing *The Space Between*

Lost and Found. Thank you to the following people for your dedication, tenacity, and passion for this book:

Patricia Nelson, my amazing agent.

Allison Moore, my extraordinary editor.

The entire team at Bloomsbury, including: Jeanette Levy, Anna Bernard, Erica Barmash, Beth Eller, Brittany Mitchell, Jasmine Miranda, Ksenia Winnicki, Phoebe Dyer, Faye Bi, Valentina Rice, Alona Fryman, Donna Mark, Diane Aronson, Stacy Abrams, Nick Sweeney, Melissa Kavonic, Nicholas Church, Daniel O'Connor, Mary Kate Castellani, Annette Pollert-Morgan, Cindy Loh, the sales and rights teams, and everyone else who has supported my books.

Thank you to Leo Nickolls for his beautiful cover.

I'd also like to thank Jana Mitchell, RN-BSN, for her insight into Cassie's mom's form of the illness.

Last, thank you to Summer, Sean, and Ross; every day I'm grateful to have you in my life.